SMALL PLACES

Tiffany Allan

ISBN: 978-0-473-57942-5

Cover design by: Geoffrey Bunting

For Mum, Dad, Rose, Candice, and Zak

CONTENTS

MARIGOLDS

This is about how my mum and my sister Zoe and my girlfriend Billy and I live together, even though Mum is an alcoholic and Billy wears baggy clothes and hates all men except me, and Zoe is sad to know any of us. I work as a builder while Zoe works in a shop full of nice clothes, and Billy works as a motel cleaner. Mum doesn't work, but she used to, cleaning offices with a big vacuum cleaner on her back. Billy, Zoe and I went to school together, but I didn't see Billy there because she was younger than me and kept her hair short. I got kicked out because they said I was taking too long to get my qualification (which made Mum call up my teacher and call her a uppity bitch which meant I couldn't even get in the dumb class the next year), and Zoe got kicked out for fighting with a girl.

When Zoe came home that day, with dark scratches down her face, Mum got real angry.

"How many times have I told you?"

"Headbutt backwards, mash her teeth," Zoe repeated.

It was too late because she and the other girl had been kicked out and anyway that would have been Zoe's name known in town. We don't have any other family to back us up. It's just us. I had a dad who came to visit sometimes but he didn't meet me until I was eight and so we were just sort of friends who hung out at McDonald's every so often until I got too old for it. Zoe's never met her dad.

When they asked my mum at the hospital after she'd given birth to me what my name was going to be she said she wanted to think about it. But they wouldn't let her leave without filling out a birth certificate. So she called me James, after my father, even though she left the father part of the certificate blank. "Never put anything in writing that you might regret later," she always tells us.

James is an easy name at least, not like my girlfriend Billy who could be either a girl or a boy's name and it doesn't help she has her hair curly and flopped on top of her head and wears a grey sweater most of the time; from behind she really could be a skinny boy.

"Look at my wrists," Mum always says, when she's had a couple wines. "They never changed size, not when I was pregnant, not even when my ankles puffed up." She's proud of being thin but I don't know why because she's in a wheelchair and her skin is grey. I can't remember if it was grey before her accident, if it's the smoking, or if it's something medical to do with her having a catheter and a bag she has to empty. It's like her body has died and is waiting for her to catch up, but she's got us to look after as she always says, so she doesn't.

Mum's in a wheelchair because she got in a motor-bike accident with her last boyfriend and he died. After she got out of hospital we went to his grave with me bouncing her wheelchair over the ruts, and she and some of her friends drank out of a cask, and Mum said, "that's the last one," and never got another boyfriend and never had any more kids. A lot of people are afraid of my mum and don't want to come over, but there's a part of the world that she fits into and the people who do come over fit into it with her. Those sorts of people drank out of the cask with her at her last boyfriend's grave.

Billy's not afraid of Mum. Not because Billy's intimidating or anything but because I don't think it much occurs to Billy to be afraid of things. She wears baggy clothes and never smiles and when men smile at her on the street she doesn't even pretend to get along with them, she just stares back. She's an artist. Mum thinks Billy's paintings are stupid because when they're finished you can't see what was in them. You feel like there might have been something there, before she started pouring thick paint over it, but that it's been ruined.

Mum's never told Billy that, only me. She doesn't get snappy with Billy, even though Mum often gets mad over little things, like when checkout girls shove her groceries in the bags too hard. I get embarrassed on those days because I like checkout girls, they're nice and they try hard with their makeup and you can tell she's making them nervous. Mum tells me I'm going to be a sucker, that at least Billy knows how to look after herself. I think she's glad that Billy makes people uncomfortable. She always looks at Zoe when Billy gets up and moves away from men, like she's saying, "learn something."

Billy's not even a little bit embarrassed about being a motel cleaner and doesn't try to dress nicely like Zoe does. Zoe only buys her clothes from the expensive shop she works at. Sometimes I drive past Billy's motel in my truck and look for her up in the balconies of those fancy rooms, with her apron straining against the wind. She's skinny but she's strong, she clatters around with a broom and holds big bags of laundry to her chest with her long arms like she's wrestling giants. She's told me about the sticky semen up the shower walls that she has to punch off with a rag, and the little flies painted on the urinals for men to aim at. I think I'd actually kill anyone who upset Billy.

I don't know what Billy's like at work, if she talks much, but they seem to like her. They all wave out to her if I pick her up, and they laugh and throw the rubbish sacks on the back of my truck and make me drive the hundred metres to the rubbish cubby, so they don't have to all walk it down there in a line of girls with brown sacks.

Mum's friends came over to visit at lunchtime today and they brought her some wine like everyone does when they come here, even though there's a sign on the door asking people not to bring alcohol into the house. Zoe was out with her friends.

"Why's James getting so fat?" Mum's friends asked when I let them in, and she smiled with her teeth because she's the one who cooks for me. Mum's friends sat around drinking wine from the box and I did wheelies on her wheelchair while Mum lay on the couch and closed her eyes and ignored all of us. Her catheter bag stuck out the bottom of her shirt and she didn't try to cover it.

Mum's friends left early because she wasn't talking much, and then she and I watched TV.

At 11 p.m. she looked up at the clock. "Go and find your sister," she said.

Because I'm the boy it's always lift this, carry that, open this, close that, go find your sister. It gets me so riled up and I ask Billy if we should move out but she always says no, that Mum and Zoe need me. Billy likes Mum. She says she wished she had a mum that strong, who protected her children like ours does.

I went to pick Zoe up in my truck. When I found her she was wandering on the cliffs above the lake, holding a bottle of wine by the neck with her fingertips. When I pulled up next to her she said, "what if I jump?"

The lake was thick and black like oil.

"Yeah, but Zoe," I said. "I've just gone and got this whole bucket of KFC."

"Give it to Mum," she said. Then she looked nervous. We both knew Mum would poke at the chicken, say it was slimy and why did we talk her into it. Then she'd eat some of the skin. I'd eat most of the rest and Zoe would take some to work tomorrow in a sandwich, for her hangover. Thinking about work made Zoe stop having fun anyway and she got in the car.

When we got home Mum looked at us suspiciously while Zoe tried to take her shoes off at the door, leaning too far over and bumping up against the wall. Mum rolled her eyes. "May as well have a wine then," she said. She was grumpy because the chicken was cold and it took too long to find Zoe, to get her in the car and not over the side into the lake, plopping like a little stone.

Zoe refused the glass of wine mum poured. I could tell she was having one of her wanting to be better than us moments, even though she was also glassy eyed drunk. They both sat in their chairs and glared at the TV, Zoe ignoring the glass in front of her and Mum drinking twice as fast to make up for it.

"Just going to waste it?" Mum asked, watching Zoe delicately scissor meat from one drumstick with her knife, mix it in with coleslaw. The bucket with the rest of the chicken sat on the bench, sweating. I jumped up and grabbed another piece.

"Not that hungry," said Zoe.

"We can drop you at the hospital then. Put you on a drip with the other skinny girls." My mouth fell open and I looked at Zoe. Sometimes Mum still shocked me, even though I knew her real audience was the awareness Zoe brought into our house, the feeling she conjured of someone else watching us, appalled. Zoe was ignoring me and staring back at Mum with her eyebrow up and a little smile on her face so I knew she was going to go in for it.

I knew better than to get involved. Every time there's an argument I notice Mum watches *me*, as if *I'm* going to do something. She's said she doesn't care what any girl says to me I am not to touch them, ever. As if I ever would.

It'd be like mashing a bug.

So I went to bed. Drunk arguments always sound stupid from the outside. Billy was already asleep when I got there and there was one of Mum's rings on the bedside table. Mum must have given it to her, which meant Mum was way more drunk than she was letting on. This happened sometimes. Billy always left them out for me and I always put them back in Mum's jewelry box. Zoe would be horrified if she knew.

I could still hear Mum's voice, loud and nonsensical. Zoe's must have been filling in the quiet parts. Eventually a car pulled up outside.

All ok? I texted Zoe.

Yeah, she replied. *Jared's picking me up. I'm going to move out.* Zoe's boyfriend. She'd been talking about moving in with him for a few weeks now. His house wasn't even that far away, like five streets.

When I woke up, the house was quiet. Billy was at work and Mum was in the lounge having a smoke. "Thought I'd go see if Zoe needs a hand with moving anything," I said.

"Well, she can come home for dinner, if she wants." said Mum.

I took my truck to Jared's house. Zoe was in the driveway when I got there, with one gardening glove off and one on. She was crying and I wondered if she might have a cask of wine on the go under the sink like Mum sometimes did. Jared was at work.

"He told me if I didn't like it, I should do something to make it better, or leave," she said.

I could imagine it. Zoe arriving late at night to a house that looked almost exactly the same as the one she'd left. She'd have been up early, pulling up bedspreads before Jared could even finish his morning coffee. Then she would have been out ripping weeds from the front of his house in great armfuls with people walking past to school and work, before giving up and curling into a horrified ball on the couch, staring at the grease-stiffened curtains. I knew because she did the same at our house.

"I thought if I just made it look nice," she said. She was still crying. She couldn't decide what we should fill the truck with, the plant rubbish or her stuff to move back to Mum's.

"I always liked those orange flowers." I said. Zoe had had flower boxes outside her old room which she would not allow anywhere else but directly outside her window.

"Marigolds. Slugs eat them and they go all shitty." She wiped her nose. "But I could get some ground cover. Morning Glory." She eyed me sharply and then smiled herself. "It's a weed, but. Grows fast. Purple flowers." She put her other glove back on and lifted an armful of hairy dandelion plants. A long-legged spider scampered out of the stems and across her shoulder. She turned her face towards it, blew it away.

I stayed most of the morning and we took a couple loads of stuff to the dump and then I went to pick Billy up from work. I invited Zoe along for dinner at Mum's, but she wanted to stay there and make a go of it, cook dinner for Jared, show him she wasn't crazy.

So it was just me and Billy who walked up to the front door of the house for dinner. It was bucketing rain by then and Billy had stopped on the edge of the road. Mum was watching us turn up through the window. Billy was crouched down next to a dead cat in the rain checking for a collar, and I was standing behind her and Mum was watching us from inside her twitched apart curtains. Billy's grey sweater was getting wet and Mum's face looked screwed up from the window, looked afraid and angry at Billy's floppy hair plastering down in the rain and me standing there, doing nothing, letting them both be. I kept hearing wheels squishing through the mud and thinking maybe someone was going to stop, someone was going to say something, but it was just more cars passing by.

SISTERS

"They suck the calcium from your bones you know," said Meg, edging the car into the slow vehicle lane. A grey truck slid past.

Ainsley spoke up from the back. "Carly lost three teeth."

Tilly, in the passenger seat, nodded.

The three sisters were on their way to the city for Tilly's abortion. Tilly's boyfriend Matt had wanted to come with them but the girls had said no. He'd been on and off the fence about the whole thing. Wishy washy. Tilly told her sisters that he'd accepted it, he'd told her it was okay. But on Friday he drank with the boys at the workshop and got swept up in the idea of being a working dad like them, with a tyke and dinner at home. He sent her messages like, *would have been cool though. A mini-us running around.* After Tilly told Meg about that, Meg called Ainsley. They both organised the time off work.

When they pulled up outside Tilly's rental Matt didn't come to the front door. The girls sat in the car and watched as Tilly came out alone in her sweatpants with a small bag.

So what? Thought Meg. But she knew she felt defensive. Were they too quick to whip Tilly off into the car? Should they have sat down with Matt, given them another week? Of the three of them, Tilly was the only one who had liked babysitting as a teenager; the only one who had kept her friends after they'd had babies and made the effort to go and see them or invite them around, kids and all. But surely earlier was better, while anonymous cells divided and multiplied.

"I'm pregnant," Tilly had said to Meg. She'd laughed a little after she said it, like *oh fuck I know right*, but then a tear had slid out. Meg had chosen her next words as carefully as footsteps through virgin snow. She'd known even then that she would be looking back on the conversation, examining the marks she'd left.

"Ah. Shit. What do you...?"

"I don't know yet."

"Have you told Matt?"

"Yeah. He's happy but also knows I might not..."

"How long have you got to decide?"

"Not long. A month or so."

Meg thought of her ex fiancé. His parents had had beautiful cats, Siamese. She thought of how he'd told her he wanted kids, all of a sudden. How he'd threatened to leave without them. She'd called their mother, not dead yet, asked her all the questions she could think of. After that Meg had drawn up a contract of sorts. *I will have kids if I can have two weeks off a year. If I can take them to my mum's anytime I like. If I can still work. If I am allowed to make jokes about them. If I don't have to take them grocery shopping. If you never call me a bad mother.*

She'd written it, in a letter. It had taken her a week. She'd meant it. Given it to him. Remembering that, Meg felt guilty for her reaction to Tilly. She had been so close herself to trying out a normal life.

He'd read it and replied, in a letter of his own.

You know, you want all these things. To settle down. Get married. Have kids. I want to travel.

"What a shithead!" Tilly had crowed, laughing, when Meg had turned up on her doorstep. "He was just looking for a reason to leave you!"

After that humiliating breakup the girls had all been single for a short special time and they'd spent their first Christmas alone together in years. They'd sat on the back porch in the sun with their long legs out and they'd drank wine and toasted their parents. They'd laughed loudly at the mean things that happened in the world and at their ugly cats zipping across the lawn. Three little girls sitting in front of a fire with long hair drying down their backs waiting for their parents to brush it now sat in lawn chairs without their parents and tied back their hair into knotty ponytails and did not need to let anyone else in.

Tilly decided not to keep it. It was the only decision, but it was hardest for her. She'd really thought about it. She'd brought down from the attic boxes of baby clothes their mother had left them, touched the wool with her fingers. She'd read articles. She'd talked to current mothers, who'd struggled in laden with baby carriers and gripping the arms of toddlers. Meg, living in Tilly's spare room *(what right do I have to discuss this, the sour bitch in the back room?)* heard a lot of the conversations.

"You won't regret it," they said.

"It's different when it's your own," they said.

The babies screamed. The older children ran in and out, touching things.

"You think you do, but you don't really know love until you've seen your own child," one said.

Meg tore that mother apart after she left. She was desperate for Tilly not to feel as hurt as she did. *Don't know love.*

Their own mother had always been off to the SPCA to pick up the oldest and ugliest cats. She brought them home with limps, wet coughs, missing eyes. She gave them a warm home for a few years and then put them down. The girls grew up to do the same. They each had animals buried all over their backyards. There was satisfaction in a clear end in a calm place with clean walls and kind people. "Our family just loves putting down animals," Meg said once, laughing, to her ex.

"Your family is all fucked in the head," he'd said.

His family had had formal Christmases, the siblings all polite to each other over ropy trifle; making plates to cajole into their kids' mouths and soft suggestions to their own aging parents. All of them pretending Christmas was a special time every year, that the world wouldn't swallow them up. That they could count on each other no matter what.

In the end the extra research, the touching of soft wool, made Tilly cry so much in the doctors' offices that they signed her off immediately. The crying convinced Matt too, for the most part. Even with his careful support Tilly still threatened to leave him, sometimes screaming, in the weeks leading up to the appointment. In the end he felt fear and surrendered her up to her sisters.

They'd split the trip into two sections, one town to another for a night, then to the city. When they got out of the car at the midway point, Meg saw the beginnings of a swell in Tilly's T-shirt.

Give me a pizza, she thought. *I'll have the same.*

The hotel room was calming. Tilly and Meg had both been hotel cleaners, knew the circuit of jobs as they entered the door, and they relaxed in familiarity. When they had worked at the same hotel they weren't allowed to clean together because they'd turn up the stereo and kick off their shoes; make themselves large cups of hot chocolate to drink while they worked. They'd been younger.

The bedspreads in this hotel were pink and orange. The girls pulled towels from the bathroom to lie down on top of them. They knew how rarely the spreads were washed. Ainsley put the kettle on and started calling out the names of the teas.

"Fuck it," said Tilly, getting up. "I'm having a drink." She clattered the car keys off the glass coffee table into her hand. She stared at her sisters.

Meg went with her. Ainsley stayed behind to have a bath. They stopped at a Thai restaurant and got Ainsley, a vegan, a tofu dish. Then they went to McDonald's and picked up a family pack for the two of them, laughing at the four cokes, and went to the liquor store. Tilly was going to get a cask but Meg worked full-time so she bought them better wine instead, a bottle each.

The three of them sat around the small round glass table in their red upholstered hotel chairs. "It's just cells," said Ainsley. Ainsley didn't usually drink. But she poured one for herself. They didn't clink glasses, but they all finished a large first mouthful together.

When Tilly started crying it wasn't even about the baby. She'd been scrolling on Facebook while they ate and caught a video on veal calves, birthed into nets so they didn't spoil their jelly texture by taking a first step.

Ainsley, who had seen the videos all before, gave Tilly a hair tie. Tilly sat on the lid of the toilet and cried.

"I ate McDonald's," she said. Meg hid a smile.

"Spew if you need to," Ainsley said.

"It'll be a waste," Tilly wailed. Ainsley and Meg caught eyes, mouths twitching.

Meg wondered if she should tell Tilly that she could back out. They wouldn't say anything. They'd be kind to the kid.

"You know what I'd love to do?" said Ainsley, breathlessly. "You know those anti-abortion people? The ones who stand outside?" Tilly looked up. "I'd love to throw some abortions at them."

Tilly slid off the toilet seat. Meg sank down the side of the door frame. They laughed and laughed. Meg imagined how hard, how horrible they would look to anyone else.

The next morning they woke up early. "Do you feel okay?" Meg asked, mindful now of not being *too h*ard.

"Yeah. I do. I feel a bit bad about that wine—"

"Jesus, I've seen people drink more than that and they *know* they're keeping them," said Ainsley.

"And the ones who try to kill it *with* alcohol," said Meg, thinking of a girl she'd met at a bonfire, who'd told her she'd drink until it died. Meg saw her around sometimes, kids in tow.

"At least you're doing it properly," she finished.

"Yeah," said Tilly. "And it wasn't even a whole bottle."

They were silent. Tilly looked as if she was about to say something else, but didn't.

When they got to the clinic the process got them in and out quickly. The nurses were all cheerful. One of them wore a black surgical cap with bright red chillies on it. They pattered while they pierced and they touched Tilly's arms and back like old friends, walking with her down the hallway. Meg was grateful to them. She and Ainsley waited. Meg kept thinking of Ainsley's horrible joke about throwing abortions and smiling, that painful ghoul smile that you cannot stop.

Forty-five minutes later they were in the car.

"What was it like?" Ainsley asked.

"It was okay," said Tilly. "Better than I thought."

"Did anyone say anything mean?" asked Meg.

"Nah. They had to ask if I was sure. But that was it."

"Is it sore?" asked Ainsley.

"Kind-of. They gave me a giant pad." Tilly laughed.

Meg nodded. What could a child do, alone, with only the three of them to watch over them? They would not risk finding out.

"I did ask the nurse though, where they put them," said Tilly, needing to say it. "I asked if, you know, they go in the rubbish bin."

"Do they?"

"Nah. They cremate them. They're treated with respect. You know."

"That's good," said Meg.

Ainsley was driving now. She whipped around corners, passed other cars at 140km. She went faster and faster. Her sisters let her. It was just how she drove.

They stopped at the same hotel, drank a shitload. They all felt lighter. Tilly didn't cry.

Tilly felt better the next day and she drove them home. They stopped at another McDonald's and then parked up at the lake, where the boy racers sat idling. Tilly parked like shit, as usual. She wound her window partway down, stretched back on her seat with her sunglasses covering most of her face and held fries out the gap in the window. Sparrows flew up and took them from her fingers.

"Would you guys have considered it?" asked Tilly, watching the sparrows. "Keeping it?"

"Nah." said Ainsley.

"Nah." said Tilly.

Meg wondered if Matt would stay with Tilly, or if he would keep looking at her empty belly. Ah well. It was done now. The three sisters wound up their windows, drove away.

LUCKY

Marie opened the door.

"Got a present for you," said one of the officers. Daniel was held up between them on the doorstep. His head was hanging down. There was thin vomit down the front of his shirt.

"Fuck's sake," said Marie.

"Where do you want him?"

Marie went back into the house. The policemen followed her, lifting Daniel over the stoop. Daniel gurgled and tried to hit one of them. They bumped him down the hall and into the bathroom. Marie held back the bath curtain.

"Put him in there".

The policemen dropped Daniel into the tub and followed Marie back to the front door.

"Where are you going?" She asked. "Can I have a ride?"

"Stay home," said one of the officers, pleasantly. "Look after your husband."

Marie didn't stay home. She left Daniel a towel and a bucket and drove into town. She knew he wouldn't remember if she'd been there or not anyway.

She met up with Shirley at the pub and they had a great time, drinking house wine and dancing, throwing their heads back. They danced to the good songs and then sat outside while Marie smoked and argued loudly with the men at the other tables. "They love that stuff," she told Shirley. When the pub closed Marie drove them home, dropping Shirley at her small unit on the way. Shirley said she should stay but Marie said no. She liked to drive out to her house in the country, when the stars were always out in their thousands. Shirley worried about accidents but Marie knew to worry about something was to attract it.

Daniel was still in the tub when Marie got home. That was fine with her. His snores swelled through the house and the cats looked at her in worry while she poured herself a last glass of wine and played her favourite songs on repeat, swaying on the breakfast stool.

In the morning Daniel was in bed with Marie and he smelled. She resolved not to look after him and left, banging the front door.

Shirley was out on the step having a coffee when Marie got to her house. Shirley had given up smoking because she'd had a cancer scare a while back and then her mum had died of it. Bad luck, thought Marie. Marie's own family were all smokers but they just went on and on with their dry mouths and bony hands. Marie lit a smoke and breathed deep.

"How's the head?" she asked.

"Bad."

"Not like you, going out all night."

"Bad mammogram," said Shirley. That was just like her, to land it on Marie like that. Marie didn't ask anything else. You didn't ask, you just waited to be told. Marie tapped some ash into the garden and looked out at the street.

"*Shirley.*" A voice from the back of the house. The voice was soft, wasting. Shirley's face dropped. It was her husband.

"I haven't told him," she whispered. Marie nodded, unable to breathe.

"I'll wait in the car," she said, and almost ran to it. Shirley's husband horrified her. He had been large and hairy and tanned once and Marie had even found him quite attractive. The four of them all used to have drunken barbecues, sitting on the grass together like teenagers. Then Shirley's husband broke his back out logging and now he lay in bed all day, calling out in a humiliated voice when he was desperate enough to know what was going on in the front rooms and outside the front door. Marie touched the crystal hanging from her rear view mirror. Quartz. She never went into his room to visit. She held onto the memories of the barbeques when the sun was out and the drinking had been fun.

When Shirley came out of the house Marie opened the passenger door for her from the inside. A dent made it stick because Marie had drunkenly slid into a culvert a few weeks ago but no one had been hurt.

When Marie pulled up next to Shirley's empty car in town the shops were all open. It was sunny and people walked past them in tights and sandals.

"Let's have a look?" Shirley asked. Marie thought about saying no but instead they went into a clothes shop. Shirley went straight for the back corner, filled with sequins and yellows. Marie hung back and looked at the salespeople, at their cool black skirts. She fingered a blouse.

"What do you think?" Shirley asked. She had on a green dress. Marie thought of barbecues. It looked like it would cheer Shirley up. A saleswoman bustled past and Marie saw themselves through her eyes. Two old women weighed down with rings and bracelets, trying on long dresses. Marie wondered if any of Daniel's spewy smell had gotten on her.

"It's your choice," she said, distancing herself from Shirley. Shirley bought the dress and Marie got in her car before Shirley could suggest going out for brunch, could try and convince Marie into pretending they belonged there on a Saturday morning.

Marie went back home alone and made herself a coffee. She trickled in some spiced rum and thought about Shirley. That much bad luck couldn't be for nothing. Shirley tried to keep a job and baked ugly sunken cupcakes for SPCA campaigns. She didn't smoke and she kept the house clean for a husband who couldn't see it past the bedroom door. Marie felt anxious, like Shirley's luck was catching. She added a little more rum and sat up straighter. She couldn't help but think a little positive thinking could go a long way for Shirley.

In the lounge Daniel was playing the Xbox in his underwear, the bare skin of his legs and back leaving wet marks on the leather. Marie joined him with her coffee and they ordered pizza. After lunch they started drinking again. It was *Saturday,* after all.

By late afternoon they'd goaded each other into a fight. Daniel lost heart first, winding down from loud shouting to red-eyed whingeing and pouring Jack Daniels into his mouth like it would make Marie try to stop him. Instead Marie went to the pantry and pulled out all the Tim Tams and chips while Daniel muttered into his chest. After glancing around the door at him Marie opened the freezer and took the frozen sausage rolls as well. Daniel would just eat them in a drunken stupor and not remember it, and she'd come home to crumbs and nothing nice for herself.

Marie put the food in her car and drove to Shirley's house.

"Let's go out for dinner! My treat!" Shirley was hesitant but Marie knew she'd go with her because she never got to go out for dinner anymore. She took Shirley to an Indian restaurant and Marie drank a bottle of wine while Shirley ate and looked all around them. Their bill came quickly.

"They're so *fast.*" said Marie.

"Should I drive?" asked Shirley.

Marie drove. Halfway through town the gas light came on and she swerved into a station, causing Shirley to spill half the stuff out of her purse which she'd been digging in for painkillers for whatever ache she had now. Marie got out and filled the car, turning around from the spigot with her finger already on the pump and spilling petrol all down one side of the door. Shirley was scrabbling on the floor mat for painkillers in a way that was making Marie feel tearful and angry so she hurriedly dropped her off and headed for home. She felt much better. That was the difference between her and everyone else, she decided. Marie was positive and she looked after herself, she didn't expect anyone else to do it.

Marie drove, coasting. The stars rolled over her bonnet. She tapped her foot to the stereo. She thought about how Shirley always went home to her husband despite everything. She turned the stereo up louder.

At the last intersection there was a dark heap sitting half over both lanes of the road. It looked like an animal watching her come. Marie took her foot off the accelerator and let the car creep forward. It was Daniel's heavy Ford, facing her. Its lights were out. She thought of Shirley's husband whispering for her. Marie felt sick. She got out of her car and walked carefully to the side window.

Daniel was in the driver's seat with his hands in his lap and his mouth open. He was breathing with wet heaving breaths. He didn't move when she shook him, only choked and snored again. He had come looking for her.

Marie looked down the empty road for a long time. Daniel had been pushing it lately. His attitude would soon attract bad things. She shut his door, wiping her fingerprints off the handle with her sleeve. If there was an accident, or the police came... Luck was precious, not for wasting on others. She got back in her car and idled past the scene.

She wondered if she had baking paper for sausage rolls.

AT THE PUB

*(Previously published
in Antipodes)*

At the pub they say, "his new missus has him whipped." Or,
"how is she with the dishes?" Or,
"they're either hot and they can't cook or they can cook but they're crazy."

The girls are sometimes there, sitting on their phones, messaging their mums or their friends far away. Or they're chatting to each other about kids. Or they're just at home, unwilling to make small talk. They'll be watching TV. Doing dishes.

Sometimes one of the women at home will call, looking for her husband. She'll call his phone, the phones of his friends. The men put their phones on the tables next to their beers to watch them light up and buzz. If she's well-known, she'll call the pub itself. By then the one who is hiding begins to look pale.

Not often, but occasionally, one of the women will go to a different pub to the one her partner is at. She'll laugh with her girlfriends if she has any, or whoever she's scraped up from around the area to join her. She'll order the syrupy pub versions of the colourful town cocktails she used to drink. But everyone in the area knows each other and it doesn't end well. "Sorry mate," the boys say. "She was too pretty to be trusted."

The men talk about dogs. Dead ones, usually. One shepherd tells how his best bitch held mobs of sheep for minutes at a time, with only a stare. How she knew what "shake it," meant, could kill a ram like *that*, but would let the farmer's own chubby daughter pull her tail, poke her fingers in her eyes. But if he'd said "shake it," while his daughter was clambering through the bitch's fur, *well*.

They talk about tractors, dirtbikes, fertiliser and grass seed and who is ordering too much and who isn't ordering enough. The girls who are there sit in silence, with nothing to offer. They wonder what would happen if they interrupted. If they said, *Hey, guess what, I had to fix a mistake at the cafe and send back some coffee today.* But it would be too awful to be ignored, ridden over and buried under their disinterest.

The men talk about bosses. Who is disorganised. How they, lowest on the chain, suffer for it. How they would have organised it instead. They talk about who loves money. Who loves to stop for breaks. Who keeps them working long after the sun has set, with headtorches. They talk about managers who are kind to their dogs. Those who don't feed their dogs enough. Those who ruin a dog with beating so that when they call to it after the day is done it lopes away from them against the fence line, tongue out, eyes rolling until they shoot it and it becomes another hero dog story.

They talk about other people in the pub. The townies—that is, anyone wearing dress shoes, anyone with skinny arms, anyone with glasses, anyone wearing a colourful woollen hat. The skiers. Anyone talking to foreign girls — who they call the honeys but never talk to. The tourists and the farmers cross over in the same places, but they don't sit at the same tables. The farmers hunch their red shoulders and mutter about the soft townie boys who can go over and talk with the honeys with long legs. They flex their big hands.

Sometimes the foreign girls aren't wearing bras. The boys stare. They point for their friends. The girls go to the bathroom and come out with jackets on, heads down and cheeks flaming.

They talk about jobs that need to be done. Jobs that will never get done. Fights they've had. They tell the same stories word for word because the others will pick up on inconsistencies like ravens. No one wants to be known as a young fella. Everyone knows young fellas tell yarns. They stick to the truth. The time one of them got locked out of the pub by the staff because if he had gotten in there, he would have gone *nuclear*. The time one of them got arrested. The time two of the boys at the table fought each other. They tell that one gently, with humor. Don't trust sluts, the two boys say. They touch bottles.

They tell the story of one of the old block managers getting knocked out, in this very bar, right over there. One of the bar staff had knocked him to the ground, and then some of the boys had jumped in and kicked him. He'd been annoying people, drunk. The boy who knocked him down was a young fella, showing off. The ones who kicked him had just been upset with all the loud noise. They tell the story with toughness, with confusion. The women listening wonder, why didn't you stop it? Wasn't he your friend? But they don't say anything.

The boys are invited more than once to have some of the food someone has ordered for the table. "Dig in," is not enough. After, "get into it boys," someone takes the first chip. The girls order their own food, impatient with the etiquette. One of the boys is having a lean week. He is careful that he does not eat the food, does not drink from any of the jugs on the table. He goes up quietly and buys his own pints.

Sometimes the girlfriends really get along. They drink wine, talk to each other. They've been lonely this week. Most of the time though they're just tired. They have jobs talking to people all day, in hospitality, in teaching, at the liquor store, the only options available. They come to the pub and just listen. To be out of the house is sometimes necessary. To be quiet is a relief.

One of the women is at home. She is looking at the box of linen that has not been unpacked since they moved in. She is wondering whether she should go out and sleep with someone else, a vagrant, a traveller. Her children are turning over in their sleep. The dishes are not done. The dog whines at the door, wanting her husband to come home. The wife pulls the door open, pushes the dog out with a kick that does not land and the dog runs away, low to the ground, tail scooped in under his body. She throws the dirty pots and pans one after the other out into the rain. If her young husband walks past them when he gets home she will leave him and go to the city. If he brings them inside and puts them back on the bench she will leave him and go to the city. She walks out to the chiller behind the house in the dark and pulls apart some briskets to defrost for the dogs. On her way back she picks up the dishes, wiping off the wet grass. They will need them in the morning.

ROME

Anna never had the guts to go back to the doctor but that was okay because she'd lived in the same town for thirty years and knew everyone. She knew the women with postnatal depression, knew cleaners and arborists with chronic injuries, even someone who was hit with a car on purpose in the main street. She knew the girls from school who had seemed fine but then one day stood in the middle of the road with a robe flapping open. They were people she had sat with at the back of high school classrooms drawing stick figures in each other's books; when Anna was young and thought she might travel to Rome, where colossal women traded filthy curses with tanned men, laughing loudly and sunning their vast bodies on the beach.

Some of the people Anna contacted after she'd been too shy with the doctor were boys (men now) she had once made out with at teenage parties, when she was not really that drunk, when the skinnier girls had been leaning over the back fence and spewing. The boys would lean back and shrug their shoulders at her and she'd always nod and step forward for as long as it would last. That was long before the girls had all sobered up, cemented their partners and had children.

Anna went to visit her old schoolmates (not the men without their women at home, small town revenge went hard) for cups of tea. She mentioned feeling down, the closest she could get to explaining the horrifying emptiness, feeding it into some patter about menopause and having a sore back.

"They don't do anything," said one old friend, one of the postnatal ones, dropping valium from a snaplock bag into her palm. "I take two or three at a time and you don't get any sort of high. You can have them."

Another friend who had come off his motorbike a few years ago and dragged himself off the road with the exposed muscles bulging out of his leg gave her a box of oxycontin. "Too addictive," he said, shaking his tattooed head. "Missus won't let me take them." The missus, next to him, nodded.

"I took these out of my son's room," said the closest friend Anna had, an alcoholic who Anna drove home often, her phone light glowing suddenly in the early hours. She put coloured pills in Anna's hand. "They're probably just some sort of shitty speed."

"I can pay you," said Anna.

"No," said her friend. "He shouldn't leave them lying around." She laughed. "Hopefully you get a kick out of them." But Anna only wanted them for things like getting up, doing the dishes.

At work Anna's boss called her aside.

"Barbara said you're too slow." Anna could not think of a reply. "If you can't keep up, we'll have to put you in for unpaid training."

Anna went back to the sandwich line. Beside the chiller she could see Barbara watching her, a stopwatch in her hand.

On night shifts Anna worked with her favourite co-worker, Caitlin. "Fuck this place," Caitlin whispered as she dragged the rubbish bags past Anna. Coke dribbled out over the tiles behind her.

"That much lettuce?" asked a customer at midnight. "I can still see the bread underneath. Can I have a whole handful of olives?"

"I'll have to charge you more," said Anna, not looking at the camera above her head.

"Leave her alone," said a drunk man, leaning against the stacked tables. "She's just working here."

"If I'd known girls like you were here, I wouldn't have bothered going to the clubs," said another one, to Caitlin. He patted the front of his pants.

The drunk man looked at his friend. "No tummy with mine, please," he whispered. Anna looked down at her stomach and shuffled a step back from the sandwich bench.

At shutdown Anna cleaned the toilets. Someone had taken a knife to the female toilet seat, gouging thick lines out of the plastic. It could have been the girl who wasn't happy with her sandwich. It could have been Caitlin, who hated working there as much as Anna but was still young and energetic enough to resist in some small way.

At two am they finished the final mop, set the alarm. They stood outside on the cobblestones, under the glowing sign. *Bread baked fresh.*

"I'm going clubbing," said Caitlin. She was still in her uniform, her apron stuffed in her pocket. She gave Anna a hug. Anna had found the younger generation were surprisingly giving like that. "Bye."

Anna stood under the sign for a moment longer. She imagined herself with some lippy, texting a husband to tell him she'd be home late. When Caitlin disappeared into the alleyway, she started walking home.

Anna threw out the alcoholic's teenage son's pills and tried the oxycontin and the valium with a notepad next to her. The painkillers made her feel sick so she started an ongoing arrangement with the postnatal mother for the valium. Every evening she took her pill with a glass of water and a free sandwich. She did her unpaid training days, three of them. She chatted with the customers and the complaints washed over her at a shore far away. She laughed at Caitlin's impressions of them after they left.

Caitlin invited Anna to her nineteenth birthday party. Anna assumed she must have mistaken the weight of her for stability, her vacuity as something measured. She wondered briefly if it would hurt anyone to see herself like Caitlin did. At the party Anna smiled at Caitlin's grandmother and helped her in the kitchen, but the grandmother did not say much to Anna and Anna knew she was wondering why Anna was there.

Where Anna's life was. Anna went with Caitlin and her friends to a bar, but it was very loud. She got Caitlin a glass of water and some paper towels as Caitlin threw up butter chicken and birthday cake in the bar toilet and then Anna, sober, drove herself home. But she was glad she had gone. She was proud of Caitlin's spirit.

Anna took her pill when she got home and watched TV. The shadows leapt up the walls. There would be no interventions for her. She felt calm, and who could blame her? People with deliberate lives who could look at pictures of European beaches with their husbands and then book the tickets, giggling and thinking *oh, I am so naughty. Naughty me.*

Anna swam up from her slow thoughts to check her violently flashing phone. She had a text from Caitlin. "Thank you for coming to my birthday," it said. The phone went off again, in her hand. "You're cool." Anna smiled.

The next Saturday morning a group of girls about Caitlin's age came into the sandwich chain while Anna and Caitlin were working. The girls clustered around the drinks machine and Caitlin busied herself with replacing the lettuce boxes. Anna stepped up to the serving line and put her gloves on. They were probably friends of Caitlin and Anna understood more than anyone the strange politics of serving people who had been equals at school. The girls did not immediately step up but kept their distance at the drinks machine. They were whispering and giggling. Anna heard Caitlin's name and a sharp laugh from one of the girls. "Say it," one of them whispered. Anna's heart dropped in familiarity.

"Slut!" one of them called. Anna expected them to run out the door as the girls from her memory would have. But these ones were crueler. They joined the sandwich line.

Anna cut their rolls at a 45° angle with the blue handled knife that was always kept sharp. She heated their chicken fillets and filled the rolls with their salad choices. She had been intending to take her gloves off and serve them at the till as well, but Caitlin had already stepped up to it. Anna was proud but also wished she could have spared Caitlin that. Caitlin took their money and gave them their wrapped sandwiches. They all stared at her to see if there was any effect but Caitlin didn't say anything. The girls left with their rolls and walked out of sight and then came back around to look through the window. Caitlin was back to replacing the lettuce boxes. She didn't look up.

When Anna went home that night for her pill and her glass of water she didn't turn on the TV. What the girls didn't know yet was that small towns had a way of ironing everyone out so that they were all eventually the same. Anna called some of the people who had been different to her once.

The girls got shoved up against walls in bathrooms by strangers. They got held and hissed at, their bags thrown out the windows in the bus. Caitlin went back to dragging full rubbish sacks across the tiles, ignoring the Coke dribbling out behind her and laughing with Anna, while Anna sliced the bread.

GARDEN PARTIES

(Previously published in
On the Premises)

William stood by the bonfire breathing in the plastic smoke and telling himself that even if Darla was pregnant, they'd take the test on Monday so they could enjoy the weekend. He nodded at Jemma on the other side of the flames who already had a seven year old. She was probably glad to be out of the house, spending time with the friends that had stopped visiting her after the first year of motherhood. If she was anything like William she'd be considering just getting in her car when the night was over and driving into a different life.

There was heavy metal music playing in the shed. The boys had hooked up the guitars and amps and an old guy with a red face was screaming a string of swear words into the microphone while someone sat on an amp and laughed. The screeching whined in William's teeth.

Eve was lolled over in an old car seat in front of the fire with her sunglasses on and William couldn't tell if she was asleep or watching the flames. She'd spent the first half of the night throwing up into an ice cream container in the house because she'd gotten too drunk too early. A guy — William thought his name might be Jared — was standing hopefully beside her.

On top of the fire was a sewing machine, dripping plastic and stinking out the yard. Someone had thrown a box of fireworks into the fire earlier and they were still randomly going off. Jemma with the seven year old suddenly copped one, squealing and lifting her knees while the sparking gunpowder pattered against her jeans. She ran and folded over into the tray of a ute with her legs kicking in the air. That made William smile. Then he remembered Darla at her parents' house, sitting around and worrying about the not-yet-confirmed baby. He looked around his bare dirt yard and imagined it covered in plastic toys, trikes and play sets. It was easy with the smell of melting plastic everywhere. Fuck it. He strolled over and put his shoulder to the back of an engineless car he was going to sell. They didn't know about the baby yet for sure, didn't need to start saving money until Monday. The boys ran to help him and they slowly rolled the car onto the fire. The tyres caught first, melting and sagging into the embers while black smoke billowed up. Then the paint started to crack and the seats whipped into flames. The smoke curled hot and stinking towards Eve in her chair but she just kept watching or sleeping through her sunglasses with the flames in her lenses leaping up☐

They slept together of course, after the fire died down and everyone trickled away and even Jared gave up hanging around. William touched Eve on the shoulder and she stirred and he still didn't know if she'd been asleep or awake but they did it anyway, didn't even move from the car seat by the fire.

William knew that if Eve went home late or not at all her mum wouldn't care, wouldn't call the police or teach her a lesson. She was bony, noodle eating thin, not rich thin. She wore soft T-Shirts. Jandals. Never asked for rides anywhere. It hadn't occurred to any of them to date her.

Years later at his son's birthday in the same yard someone was cleaning the sputtering barbeque with chemicals and the air was rich again with the smell of toxic smoke. Eve was in front of William again, but Eve was different. She held her face in a still, small smile and she drank soda water with slices of the lime she had brought with her. She stood silently beside her husband and ignored her children who were shouting in the swimming pool. She looked proud and ugly. Darla was next to William, they'd gotten married. He could hear his son crying, being bullied by the girls in the pool. The smell lingered. He stared intently at Eve and when she looked at him he raised an eyebrow like, *look at us now, right?* But her eyes slid right off him and rested somewhere on the back fence. He raised his beer high and threw back the last mouthful and cracked another almost in the same breath, loudly, so that — he didn't know — maybe she'd realise she was being a bitch. But she just smiled at Darla and sipped her soda water.

The boys had all smiled behind their hands when Eve eloped because they knew why, she'd have been embarrassed to stand in front of them all and say *look at me now. Marriage material.* But William now watched closely to see if she was. She touched her husband's elbow to warn him that he was probably talking too loudly and she loaded plates with food for her kids serenely as if she didn't care if they ate it or not. She didn't say anything that wasn't measured or safe.

William was only 33 and in the mornings some nerve in his shoulders burned all the way down into his hands, making them tingle miserably. He listened carefully to a specialist who showed him replicas of backs and nerves and knees and got him bending down, squatting to pick something off the floor, tucking his head to get back up. He opened another beer. There were plastic toys all over the lawn. His wife hated him for the clothes he left on the couch, for pretending he couldn't hear his son crying, for the thousand other things. And even Eve had all but disappeared. He stared at her more intently. His grip on Darla's hand grew tighter and she pulled it away from him.

Eve was passing, perhaps even as someone more than the rest of them. She had travelled down to the barbeque in a nice car while her tall husband wrangled the kids in the back seat as a break from his good job. She had on a linen dress. A gold bracelet. She had slick kids that were bullying William's own. A clear voice. Did it mean they had to treat her differently? Remember the past differently?

Eve went into the house.

William followed her.

"We took out this wall," he said in the kitchen, pointing. He was expecting her to come closer to look but she just glanced at it and then looked at him. Stupid Eve, he remembered. She always had to be directed. "Do you like it?" he asked.

Darla was at the door. "What are you looking for?" she asked. "Because I've already brought everything out." She stared at William and her eyes said *I hate you*. Eve looked at them both and her eyes said nothing at all. Eve went down the hallway to the bathroom.

"The vodka," said William, staring back at Darla. "That's what." He took the bottle outside and stood next to Eve's tall husband, offering him drinks in a plastic cup.

Darla put him in the shower after the sun had set and the kids had gone to bed. She shouted about how rude he was to be badgering that slut after all this time and he wondered if she was still calling her that because she was afraid of Eve's gold bracelet as well. In the morning William woke up in his bed with the smell of smoke in his clothes and he didn't know how he got there.

MY HOUSE

I'd been dreaming that I was a child in a beautiful house watching the sunset through big glass windows. There had been fruit and chocolate on the coffee table. I'd had my little feet up on the couch cushions. Behind me the key had turned in the lock. The owners had come in with their bags, putting them down and staring. I'd realised with a sinking stone in my gut that it wasn't my house. I'd been caught.

Awake now, I get up and open the curtains. I *do* have the big glass windows. The sun is rising. I pull up the white bedspread to feel its thread count in my hands. I remind myself of what is mine.

I have an apartment with white walls
I have a $300 winter coat
I have candles and perfume, my home is clean
I have an iPhone

My iPhone is ringing.

"Wilhelmina it's reception, the rubbish collection want to know—"

"I'm very busy," I say.

"If you like we can take you through the drop off point again, at a time that suit—"

"Yes, that's a good idea." I hang up. I peep out my peephole and my little garbage bag is there. No one robs places with rubbish out the front when it's not rubbish day because they know if you're like that you probably haven't got much good stuff to sell. Rubbish by the door all the time is better than coming home and seeing you've been robbed and crawling through the soup of broken glass and the insides of your cupboards and your own clothes all over the floor.

I go through the kitchen to the bathroom and throw my socks in the toilet. I stand there for a long time looking at them, trying to figure out what's wrong. They float on top of the water. The realisation comes slowly. They're supposed to be in the washing machine. I fish them out with a toilet roll and put them in the right place. These things happen sometimes. I tip water in my handbag or I forget what building I'm in. My friends and I, we used to do things like put a rag over our faces and huff up fly spray, and I think that's why.

At work they look at me and they don't see a can of fly spray like some of the people at home would, people I work hard not to even remember. I work reception for the council of the whole city. I research all the bylaws so I know the answers and I put names to faces on the staff portal so I can call them by name when they come in through the sliding doors. On my first day I got my mum to call the front desk over and over so I could practise patching her through to all the extensions.

Everyone says that I get it. "This place would fall apart without you," they all say. When the mayor and the councillors speak I nod violently. When I do tours of the chamber for the public I spray on layer after layer of perfume so no one can ever recognise me for what I am.

I open the window of my apartment. It's cool enough outside that I can put on my winter coat. In my coat my back is straighter, my voice is clearer. I get my nails done for the same reason and eat sixteen dollar salads. More than this, I send my family big presents; giant hampers for the kids and vouchers for everyone else. Clean men in coffee meetings ask to come home with me but I say no because I don't want anyone in my house.

I leave my apartment, past my little rubbish bag, and take the lift downstairs to get a coffee from the cafe on the ground floor. I walk to work because I live right in the city, high in my apartment. I like to go early in the morning, in the club of all the other professionals walking with their coffees.

It's going to be a cold and sunny day. A motorbike gurgles up the street, the ugly sound echoing off the walls of the city buildings. The man on it is old but heavy. He has a beard and grey eyebrows. He's wearing leather and big steel toed boots. I wait with my coffee. He coasts over to me, holding up the traffic. He nods at me and I nod back.

"Come for a ride," he says. I have the key for the building in my hand. I was going to open up for the day, turn all the lights on. I have a meeting at 8 a.m. that I can't miss. I look over his head.

"You're going to get on," he says. "I can always tell."

I think about my linen lounge suite, my sheep-skin footstool. I was going to have sushi for dinner and a glass of wine and look out over the city.

The motorbike idles in my way, wet and hideous. I've been to a hundred different versions of this man's house. Casks of wine under the coffee table, clothes dry-ing everywhere. There'll be strangers like me all over the couch cushions, on the beds with no sheets, curled up in the garage in sleeping bags. Any time it feels too busy or dirty we'll just drink more, smoke more. I hold my keys tight. I will open the door of my building. I will turn on the computer. I will drink my coffee.

"They told me you'd be here," he says. He looks around. "Said you'd be trying something like this."

I stare at him. Somewhere in my beautiful house the key turns in the lock. The owners come in as if it was never mine at all. My shoulders are traitors; even in my nice winter coat they slump. My hands fall. I kneel and put my coffee on the ground. I put my keys next to it and look at them for a moment before getting back up. I'd been so close.

"Wilhelmina? Mondays amirite? Oh look, you've dropped your coffee too! Come with me — I'll shout you another."

The new mayor, a bouncing young lady who everyone said had no brain pushes her arm through mine. She dips and puts my keys back in my hand. I didn't even know she knew my name. As she swings me back toward the coffee shop I look at her but she's looking back at the man on the motorbike and shaking her head. She faces forward again and tosses her hair. "I *love* your coat," she says, giving my arm a squeeze.

SUMMER

*(Previously published
in Mayhem)*

When Sam's tree-house burned down and he went to hospital with sticky burns down the back of his legs he also had a bruise on his back that no one asked to see. His father Chris sat in the waiting room in a hot bath of red sweat. Chris's wife, Hannah, sat one full chair away from him.

By now the neighbour's kid would've jumped back over the fence and told his own parents all about it. They would've seen Chris lift Sam into the car, speed off to hospital. They'd have heard how Chris had kicked Sam before realising that Sam was already hurt, Sam was already paying. The neighbours would link this knowledge to the (*once-in-a-blue-moon for Christ's sake*) shouting over the fence when Chris lost his temper with Hannah or the kids. They'd be drawing their conclusions. Chris's face was brick red.

When Sam came out of the ward he didn't remember the kick and only wanted to show them his puffy padded legs. Hannah ran to him and held him and Chris stood up and then sat back down. He said nothing. The nurses would have seen the bruise.

It had been a hot, muggy summer. Chris worked in a sweltering trade garage with the aluminium door flung open and the sun pushing in, hitting his equipment and burning his neck. Hot bits of metal from his welding torch drifted into his clothes and left pinprick burns. When customers or his manager stood behind him and spoke while he was working, all the heat that Chris had been holding in his core flushed to the surface and burst out on his skin. His armpits stank. Down in his jeans his underwear became sodden. He spoke angry, short words until they went away.

When they got home from the hospital the house was humid and it was hard to breathe. Chris did the dishes. He hated seeing dishes on the bench. When he'd been a kid his own mother had left coffee cups everywhere, sitting in her robe and stubbing her cigarette butts into the crusty mugs while her children tried to hug her and got their ragged baby nails tangled in her greasy hair. Dust had mounded around the cups and shit caked puppies had licked bowls on the floor. They'd had a wire netting fence and anyone could see Chris and his siblings grow up from the road.

He pulled the shade, getting dish bubbles on the mesh.

Hannah watched Chris from the doorway, Sam's hand in her own. She wouldn't let his hand go. The steam rose from the water in the sink and sweat trickled down Chris's back. Mosquitoes sucked at his feet, sticking agonising probes into his skin.

"Are you okay?" asked Hannah. He knew he couldn't answer her without shouting. It wasn't her fault. It was the heat. He nodded, shook his head, dumbly, anything to get her away from him, fuck *off*, and she finally, finally left, taking Sam upstairs even though Sam was saying he wasn't tired. Sam wanted to go next door and show the neighbour his padded legs. Chris clattered the cutlery louder and louder until he couldn't hear his wife and his son anymore. One of the cups broke against his palm and he nearly picked it up in his fist and stove it through the window but he carefully, carefully, wrapped it in newspaper and put it in the bin, which was nearly overflowing. *Where could he go where they might be safe from him?*

Hannah came back downstairs and went into the lounge while Chris mopped. He heard the TV turn on. She wasn't a lazy bitch but sometimes she looked it. Chris couldn't stop the hot thought from flashing in, burning out. He wondered if she might leave him for this. Hoped she wouldn't. He'd felt her leaving before. She would begin to prepare, to clear out old clothes from her stuffed closet and to leaf through property pamphlets in other towns, but in the end routine took over and she always stayed without even telling him she'd been thinking of going.

And Chris had been trying. He'd taken her to his boss's house for dinner, to meet his wife so they could unwrap salads together and murmur and the men could tip a craft beer back and watch them, knowing they were doing a good thing for their wives who sat at home alone most of the time. His boss had a tennis court and a pool. Hannah had worn a brown dress and curled her hair. He'd worn leather shoes, to take off in their foyer. They'd even thrown swimsuits in the car, just in case they all had a night time dip — *Who knew?* But it was all wrong. When they arrived with their bottle of wine Chris's boss and wife were in jeans. The boss's wife was wearing *slippers for god's sake*, and they just put the wine in the pantry and sat on the couch and watched TV. They'd ordered Chinese. The pool had lapped softly outside.

When they'd gotten home Hannah had wanted to talk about the movie they'd watched and make the best of it all but the kids had gotten into the pantry with their teenage babysitter and there was burnt sauce spilt all over the element. They were at the table frozen, watching him, their forks tangled in half cooked pasta.

Chris had walked stiffly upstairs. He'd had control, even though his abrupt departures from them cut him apart from them irreparably.

The fucking neighbour's kid. Chris finished the dishes and went to the lounge and stood behind Hannah. Her neck was corded with tension. He did not touch it. He went upstairs and checked on the children, looking in at them from their door. They slept in the same position, arms thrown up above themselves, lips sweating. He remembered being handed them as newborns, red bundles radiating heat, their damp fragile heads.

He'd done badly today. He needed more time, more privacy, to do better. He'd heighten the fence. Maybe they'd move rurally. The kids could have pets. Hannah would settle back in.

The obscene evening sun leaned against the curtains, trying to crack the house open. Chris reached above the children's heads, pulled the thick material tight.

LEMONS

When they opened their doors bright yellow lemons spilled out onto the ground. Dust, kicked up into clouds, settled in the sisters' eyelashes and hair. The coolant ticking and splashing under the hood was the only sound. Jenny sat down hard on the ground and then lay back laughing, tears sending ribbons through the dirt on her cheeks, carving rivers under her chin. Carla laughed too, leaning a hand on the driver's side door. She'd been sliding on purpose, gliding through the red sand and leaving it rolling up behind them until they'd lost control and slammed into a dune. The dogs in the tray of the ute were barking hysterically, their howls changing to yips once they could see that Carla and Jenny were okay.

Nettie would be waiting for them by now with mixing bowls ready. She'd just *scream* if she knew. The sisters patted the dust from their hair and clothes, picked up the lemons, and got back in the car. Nettie was waiting.

Nettie made a lemon cake while Jenny and Carla drank bourbon and leaned against the chipped tiled bench. Jenny and Carla pressed wine on Nettie until her cheeks flushed and she laughed with them about their lonely childhood home in the desert. They all sat down for dinner, the three sisters and Nettie's husband Joe.

Joe lit a smoke at the table and watched the girls talk and drink. He pointed to the hill behind the house. "If you wanted to," he said to Nettie, "you could run up there and back every day." Jenny and Carla looked at Nettie but Nettie just smiled into the air. They went back to ignoring him.

"Anyone want a cup of tea?" Nettie asked at the end of the night. "Peppermint is good for — metabolism."

"Black," said Jenny.

"Two sugars," said Carla.

On Nettie's way past, Carla hooked her around the middle and pulled her onto the couch. The girls planted a big kiss each on Nettie's cheek. Nettie squealed and ran to the kitchen.

The girls looked at Joe. They pulled their sleeves back over their calf dropping muscles, their tattoos.

"Nettie's fine." Jenny said.

Joe looked at his feet. He mumbled something about "...sister bitches." Jenny smiled at that, a big, raucous smile.

Nettie, somehow even bigger than before, strode back in with cups and cake.

The next day they drove to their parents' house. They

left Joe at home, he never came along anymore and no one minded. Nettie sat in the back, leaning forward to listen when Carla and Jenny spoke. The dogs shifted and jumped over each other in the tray of the truck, creating slithering and thumping sounds that fed through the back of Nettie's seat. The girls' parents lived further out in the desert than Nettie. The house was small and stained with dust but the door was open and their parents Steve and Emily came out through it as soon as the girls pulled up.

Carla let the dogs out and they leapt around barking for a minute until she whistled through her teeth and they stopped. They licked Steve and Emily's hands and then waited at the gate. Steve and Emily's own dogs barrelled out the front door.

"Jeez mum," said Carla.

"They're getting old," protested Emily.

"Wait 'til you see how much she's feeding them," said Steve.

Carla opened the gate and all four dogs fed through into the back yard. She glanced at the water trough which was full, the gauge bobbing as her dogs drank.

The house was cool and quiet. The floors were exposed wood and the kitchen and lounge were cool polished concrete with woven rugs. The girls went to the fridge and opened beers for themselves and their father. Emily had already made a pitcher of margarita and poured herself and Nettie a glass from the sweating jug. "Paul coming?" asked Jenny.

"Uh huh. Sometime." said Steve.

Carla eyed the dog hair on the couch and then sat down. Nettie plopped next to her and Emily plopped next to Nettie. She put out her hand and shook Nettie's leg affectionately.

"It's been cold at night," said Emily to Carla, running her hand over the tufts of dog fur. Carla sighed and then laughed. "She's so mean," said Emily to Nettie.

"She is," agreed Nettie. "Except for Jenny." Jenny punched her arm from where she'd been leaning on the back of the coach.

"Got a present for you guys," said Jenny to her mother. She went to the car and came back with a painted canvas. They all stared at it. It was awful, a dizzying openness of sky and dust. They knew it was the view from the back porch but it looked so empty and so lonely and so unlike how they'd grown up that no one had anything to say. They knew it would be incredibly expensive if she sold it. People paid a lot for that loneliness, for the empty chasm that came from Jenny. Emily acted quickly and full of love.

"Up here," she said, dragging a chair over to the kitchen. "Steve." Steve opened a drawer for a nail and took the hammer from under the bench. He climbed the chair and Emily handed the canvas over to him. Within moments the painting was above the sink, the emptiness already being swarmed by the red wall and the warmth of the kitchen. Nettie and Carla nodded, and Emily and Steve gave Jenny a kiss.

"Thanks love." Steve said.

Emily and Nettie drank half the pitcher and went

into Carla's old bedroom to look at fabric. Carla and Jenny went with their father out the back to the shed where they lit smokes and helped Steve to move some timber. Jenny played idly with the table vice, spinning it open and closed. When they were children they'd had competitions to see how tight they could wind it shut on their hands.

Their brother Paul pulled up at the front door in his truck. His dogs were leaping up against the sides of the cage in the back, and poured out of the tray when he opened it for them. They ran through the gate and in with the other dogs, to snarl and scuffle and follow each other around. Paul already had a beer in his hand and clinked it against Carla's when she walked out to him. They all met again in the kitchen.

"Nettie pregnant?" Paul asked the room. Nettie's face drained. Emily turned bright red.

Carla said, "Jesus Paul—"

"No!" said Nettie. "I mean—"

"You sure honey?" Asked Emily. "I thought maybe..."

"And you made a margarita?" asked Steve.

"I didn't put any alcohol in it," said Emily. "I thought I'd understood," she said to Nettie.

"Mum, I drank wine last night!" said Nettie.

"Could be," said Paul. "It's not a fat thing, Net. You look... shinier."

Now Jenny and Carla began to look.

"Could be," they agreed. Nettie went whiter.

"If I am, I won't stay with Joe," she said. They gaped. "Maybe I will. How can I know? I don't know what — will the shops be open?"

"I'll go get you a test," said Paul. "Gotta run the dogs anyway."

"I'll come," said Carla. "We'll take them all. Dad, your dogs?"

Steve nodded. Paul and Carla went out the back and Nettie leaned against the bench.

"Sorry love," said Emily.

"You reckon a gas station will sell them?" asked Paul.

"No," said Carla. The dogs thumped and churned in the back.

"Chemist then," he said. He drank out of his beer and put it back in the drink holder.

Nettie was mortified. "You're supposed to wait 12 weeks," she said. "Even if I was. You're not supposed to do it with your whole family—"

"We're just seeing if Mum can put tequila in the margarita tonight or not," said Jenny, squeezing the back of her neck. "That's all."

Nettie smiled in spite of her trembling hands.

"Going back out to the shed," said Steve, looking at Emily over the girls' heads.

"I'll come check in the— freezer," said Emily.

"You *are* looking good, Nettie," said Jenny. "Paul's a shit but I think he meant you're looking... *something*. Fuller."

"I've been—"

"You can come and live with us," said Steve, coming back in with Emily. "If you want to."

"If you want to leave Joe," Emily said. "Or separate

for a while."

Nettie didn't say anything. "Let's just wait," she said eventually.

Paul walked right up to the counter and asked to see the pregnancy tests. Carla wasn't embarrassed but she was impressed at how he valued efficiency over delicacy even in this small matter. She would have looked on the shelves by herself, even with all her dogs in the truck and her heavy boots. The pharmacist brought the test to the counter for him and he paid and they got back in the truck.

They ran the dogs from the turnoff all the way home, streams of fur bulleting up the sides of the truck and behind it, criss crossing in a black and brown current of heavy breathing and the sounds of nails scratching the dirt.

At the house the dogs flopped on the front grass that Emily laboured over with sprinklers and seed. They flung drool up over their cheeks as they drank heavily from the trough and whipped their heads back and forth to clear their noses of the water.

Nettie took her test quickly in the bathroom while everyone waited outside. They all stood at the door with their drinks, not even giving her a moment alone.

It was negative. Emily added half a bottle of tequila to the pitcher. After Nettie got drunk she showed them something.

"I can do a handstand," she said. They stared at her arms, at her body in the couch. Of course they had to see it. Jenny and Carla cleared the side tables out of the way. Paul held the oldest inside dog and laughed when it started barking at Nettie who was suddenly upside down. Jenny and Carla demanded to be shown how. Their natural strength had them up beside her but their feet banged noisily against the wall and they had no flexibility so they stomped back down. Nettie had liquid control.

"I've been learning," she said. "At the school gym. A lady started a class for adults and I thought—" she shrugged. "I can even do a vault jump," she said. Paul roared and slapped his mother's leg, spilling his beer on the couch.

After the sun went down and they ate dinner Paul and Steve dragged some full fadges of wool onto the back lawn and Nettie showed them her vault jump. They all tried it, running and tumbling in heaps while the wool puffed out the sides of the fadges and the dogs barked hysterically beside them. Paul and Steve had a go, and they all cheered on Emily who jogged up and then at the last second just patted her hand on the wool, laughing. Their shouts and the dogs' barks echoed out into the empty desert, filling it up. Jenny leaned against the porch railing and began to sketch a drunken painting filled with tangled limbs and fur and sound, swelling up to the trillion stars.

HOOVES

K aren eased the car around the bends. Melissa sat next to her in the front. They were silent, looking out their windows. Karen glanced in her rear vision mirror and he was there, in the back seat. There were fleas crawling on his chest and the hair under his armpits was matted into wet curls with sweat. He sat placidly, staring ahead, hands neatly folded in his lap. His hooves were apart, one on each side of the centre of the car. He was shirtless and his skin was dark leather where it wasn't hairy. She could smell hot salt.

Melissa stirred. "Who do you think will bring him to the church?"

"I'd say his younger brothers. I don't know which car they'd fit the coffin in though— they've got a truck —"

"Maybe no one is bringing him? He might already be there."

"Did anyone take him home?" Karen asked. Her people were colonisers and invaders, mangling and trampling beliefs from everywhere through the wet leaves of the places they forced their roots into. Some of them brought the dead home, to spend a week or a night surrounded by family and farewells. Others preferred to leave them in the morgue, saying goodbye to the air. Karen's mother was part of the miserable Irish and they saw ghosts and capering creatures in their dreams. Her father was gypsy and secretive, erasing possessions of the person gone, whether they were confirmed dead or just travelled away with the roaming beast god.

They sat in silence. The smell of sweat grew and Karen wound down her window. The goat headed man —she didn't know what to call him — *Bocanaigh? Veles? Why was he here?*—turned his head slightly to look at her. His fur ruffled in the breeze. He tapped a slow tattoo on the bottom of the car. There was no expression on his face at all.

Karen wanted to start a conversation about anything else. "A lady I cleaned with, she was telling me how her parents had the only van in the family. So they would always end up transporting the—" she paused. "Bodies — when they travelled around. She said the kids hated it; refused to sit in the back. A big painter's van."

Melissa laughed. "That was our cleaner too! She said all she could think with all the decorations and a corpse in the back was, 'what if one of my rich friends sees this?'"

They laughed, relieved, even though Karen noted Melissa had talked about her cleaner instead of a friend. There was a *whuff* of sound from the back and Melissa smiled at the mirror. A laugh? Did Melissa see him? Karen's mother probably would have. Her Grandmother, definitely.

"We never had that — you know, bringing them home or driving around with them," continued Melissa. "It was just... you turned up at church. There'd be music and the coffin would already be there. You didn't really touch it. Now that I think about it, it seems quite sad. But those have all been grandparents. Not..." She trailed off. "Surely someone would have..?" she started.

Karen said nothing. Crystal's family were hard and secretive, they pulled stiff shells over themselves. It was difficult to say what the girls would be walking into. Karen had always avoided going to Crystal's house when they were children. There had always been a feeling of electricity, and a faint smell of burnt plastic. Melissa hadn't even been allowed over there. Would Crystal's family have taken him home? Who did he belong to most?

Karen imagined the coffin sitting overnight in the dark funeral parlour waiting for them to arrive, for someone to turn the lights on.

The death of a brother. It was the worst funeral yet.

"Family trees!" chirped the teacher — a new one — who didn't know what she might be uncovering. Everyone drew branches, leaves, apples with spaces. Some got confused over dads and half siblings. Karen finished quickly. The lone apple. Her. The two leaves. Her parents. One more above her mother. Her Grandmother. She didn't even know her Grandfather's name.

"Let me help. What are your parents' last names?" She knew those of course. "What about their names before?"

How to tell the teacher that her parents had just laughed when she'd asked? *Why worry about it?* They'd asked. *Convicts and pig farmers. We're here now.*

Karen cruised around the corners. It was one winding road up the mountain and down the other through native forest, set aside in the middle of farmland. The trees and moss towered overhead, dark and tangled. They could have been anywhere. Up and up the girls went. They were both lost in thought. Karen knew Melissa hadn't seen much of Crystal since school, but she'd kept the line open for any hopeful updates from Karen, and she was there to travel with her to the funeral. Karen was grateful.

"Karen?" said Melissa eventually. "We're not going to ask about how he— you know— are we?" Karen knew what she was talking about. Crystal would just lie anyway. When the girls talked about their work Crystal always interrupted with something loud, like how she'd had a seizure in the admissions office for university and they wouldn't let her enrol. The audacity of those lies were intentional. A *fuck you* to all of them for leaving her to her own path. There had been more stories when they were younger. Crystal couldn't give Melissa's pair of jeans back because they'd been burned in a house fire. She couldn't help with their work because she'd fallen in a puddle. She couldn't bring in the money they'd fundraised for camp because her parents had used it to reconnect the phone, because when her dad went after her mum he always ripped all the phone cords out of the walls.

Karen wondered how Crystal would say Ben died. They'd all heard when he'd gotten his bike and could guess from the few options that came after, but it was better to let Crystal tell whatever lies she wanted today.

Karen suddenly breathed a deep, shuddering sigh that she didn't expect.

"Sheep!" Shouted Melissa. A mob of ragged sheep chewing grass looked up, watched the car go by.

Karen had lived rurally long enough not to peer after them but Melissa turned around in her seat to watch them disappear.

"Have you heard of the goatman?" The teacher aide had asked Karen in the staff room. He was there to take the worst students for a walk when they drew fake guns and pulled the triggers at their teachers. *Snick snick.*

"He lives in the woods. He sticks out his hoof for a ride and if you don't pick him up something bad will happen. Ask your parents about him."

The other staff members joined in.

"He doesn't speak. He carries you through where you were gonna have an accident."

"Not all the time. Sometimes he's just there for a funeral, turns up in your car on the way."

"He's a satyr, he protects —"

"No, he's a Bocanaigh, there for the violence—"

"He's half man half goat."

"He stamps on the side of the door when he's ready to get out—"

"Hangs around death."

"Never seen him? You might."

They didn't mention Veles, the gypsy beast, but Karen didn't expect them to. She didn't even know herself. In the back seat the creature shifted his leg and a plastic bag next to him moved.

They had to park around the corner when they arrived at the funeral parlour. There were cars and motorbikes everywhere, engines curdling. The men skulked around the entrance in patches and smoked cigarettes. The girls walked past them all.

Crystal started up the aisle to meet them. The girls registered shock. *But,* thought Karen, *she's always been skinny.* An older lady planted herself in Crystal's way before she got to them and gripped her hands hard. Crystal stared down at her upturned face. The stare was from a great height, as if Crystal wasn't really attending at all.

Karen knew that stare. She'd seen it the last time she'd been at Crystal's house. She had taken her boyfriend Dave there. She went into the memory, sifting, trying to avoid the reality of Crystal walking toward them without her brother.

There had been animals and woolen blankets everywhere. Karen and Dave had arrived before Crystal had gotten home and they sat in the lounge with an older guy who was waiting for Ben, Crystal's brother. Kittens had been mewling, pulling each other face over feet.

They had gummy eyes. Ben's friend was talking rapidly to no one about glove boxes and feng shui.

Dave lit a cigarette and leaned back. "Mmm-mmm," he agreed. Everyone smoked inside. The kittens plopped onto the floor and cartwheeled closer to Karen's glass of wine.

The door slammed open, really whacked into the wall, and Crystal struggled in. Ben was still absent. "Look at all this stuff I got," she said. In her long arms were clothes. She'd been at the dump. She dropped them on the floor and the kittens struggled over and wormed through the fabric.

"You want this one?" She held up a purple woolen jersey. Karen nodded and put it on. Crystal had a foot heater blasting day and night smelling of burned plastic but it did next to nothing.

"Wine?" Crystal took a swig from the bottle, acting crazier than she was, for the benefit of the stranger.

It was freezing but no one seemed to notice. Air whistled through the floor and if anyone knelt and looked through the slats they could see the dirt under the house.

"I'm out of here," Crystal was saying. "I'm getting a house in town."

A car pulled up outside. The dogs started barking. The door flew open. "Where is he?" a girl's voice shouted. Crystal started to laugh. The girl came into the lounge, started for Crystal and then changed her mind and went to Ben's friend. Karen felt for her. The girl pulled at his clothes and slapped his chest, wailing, and they both went outside. Crystal smiled at Karen and

Dave while the voices outside rose and fell. She poured more wine for Karen.

The fireplace wall shuddered. Karen and Crystal moved to the window and looked down. Ben's friend had the girl pressed against the side of the house by her face. Karen looked at Crystal to see what they should do but Crystal just stared down at them with no expression at all. The girl went limp and Ben's friend let her go.

"I can't think with you shouting at me," they could hear him saying, muffled through the wall. "You can't come in here shouting and screaming," he said. The girl was crying. She went back to her car and backed down the driveway.

Ben's friend came back inside with no explanation. Karen went back to the couch. The sun lit up the backs of the clouds behind Crystal's head. They swelled outward, rent with light. It looked like something terrible was trying to get through, some monster made of a killing brightness. Why hadn't Crystal done anything? Why hadn't *Karen* done anything? But Crystal just kept staring outwards, far away from all of them. Karen's heart beat fast. She felt like a voyeur. She'd been half in love with the idea of being Crystal, giving up on work or car warrants or the thousand other mundane things. Now it just seemed dangerous. There was a scuffling and a thump, a crash of glass. The boys jumped to their feet. Crystal paused with her lighter and her cigarette. But it was just the kittens, fallen off the table and taken Karen's wine glass with them.

Karen and Dave hadn't gone back to visit Crystal or Ben since. It wasn't that they were suddenly too good

— just that— Well. That was it, wasn't it? No other way to say it. Karen pushed the thought down.

Crystal reached the girls at the back of the funeral parlour before Karen could figure out what to say to her. When she got to them she stopped and looked hard over their shoulders and out the back door. Some of the men from the street had started filing in, standing around the back. None of them took any of the seats. A guffaw of laughter leapt in through the doors from outside and just as suddenly stopped, leaving organ music.

Karen's boyfriend Dave arrived. He'd driven over separately from work. He walked over to them, holding out bottles of water for the girls. They had condensation swelling over bright blue labels. "Take those outside," hissed Karen, for no reason.

"I'll put them in the car," said Dave, shocked and miserable. He left and before he could make it back in the coffin began its journey into the church, carried by strangers in heavy boots. Crystal stared at it. The service began. Karen knew Dave would be too polite to risk coming in late. He'd wait outside for hours.

Dave had slept with someone else but he'd been trying *so hard* to make it right. Karen had told Crystal, too embarrassed to tell Melissa that she hadn't left him. Melissa would not have stood for that. Crystal had commiserated, then suddenly grown sick of her. "Get over it," she'd said. "Or find another one."

Karen had gotten the message. Choose where you belong. Don't show me these pitiful mouthfuls of air.

Crystal didn't sit with any of her family so Melissa

and Karen took over, sitting on each side and holding a hand each as the service began. Crystal glared at Ben's coffin, back straight. They sat that way through the eulogy, the speeches — which were few, no one at the back got up to say anything. They sat through the minister saying, "unfortunately Ben's father could not be here," even though the girls had passed him on the way in, skulking with the others. Crystal had scoffed at that and two people in front had turned around to have a look at her.

There was a powerpoint display of photos. Ben's mum and younger siblings must have made it. The photos dissolved with sad music through from infancy to childhood and Karen smiled and felt her first tears form. Ben playing with water pistols in a small paddling pool. Wearing floaties at the loch. Crystal holding his hand on the beach.

None of his later photos made it into the powerpoint. As far as the women in the funeral parlour were concerned, the story of Ben's unfair life stopped as a teenager smiling, trying not to smile, one arm awkwardly loped over his body. There were no photos of his new friends, the male members of his family, of motorbikes, of him in boots. *We've taken him back now*, the powerpoint said. A hard consolation.

The service ended. Crystal didn't wait for the casket to go. She left the church with the girls trailing behind her and strode to her car with her keys out.

"You guys coming?" She asked.

Melissa had already planned for this. She didn't want to witness the next part. "No," she said, making it sound firm and caring at the same time.

But Karen couldn't bring herself to say an excuse out loud. She didn't want to go with Crystal, to watch her make whatever decisions were on her mind. But she couldn't let her go home alone. She gave Melissa the keys to the car and the hotel they'd booked for the night. She promised to meet back up with her later. They all roundly ignored the burnouts screeching up and down the street from the men, their only offerings to Ben. All three of the girls looked at each other for perhaps the last time, pretending they'd had choices to get them where they were.

Karen didn't know who she belonged with. She got in Crystal's car.

"Assholes," Crystal said about the men, as they pulled away from the pavement.

Shit. Karen had forgotten to tell Dave where she was going. She suddenly felt like an idiot. What was she doing? No wonder he avoided her. She turned around to look for him but she couldn't see his truck. She looked at the glovebox, so close to her knees. She couldn't bring herself to ask Crystal to take her back. "Do you have a family tree?" She asked, absurdly. Crystal turned her head, fully away from the road, and stared at her.

"What?"

Up until then Karen had been proud that she'd never been on the end of the stare, that they'd always understood each other, even when occasionally Melissa didn't understand them. She'd thought that they might laugh off knowing the ins and outs of one's parents.

But there the stare came, from miles up. In that

height, far above ground, Karen saw a young Crystal holding hands with Ben. She saw them running across paddocks still wet from the morning, phone cords and plaster littering the floor of the shuddering house behind them. She saw the narrow loop of Ben and Crystal's lives with one of them cushioned early in satin, right where it was a surprise to no one. Karen was a fool. She hadn't understood anything.

She wished she'd found Dave. So what if Crystal went home alone? Any story would be better than this one. Karen focused on the glovebox. She kneaded her knees. She turned around one last time at the last corner, looking for anybody— even the roaming beast — and there was Dave, right behind them. His black truck vibrated as it sped toward the back window. In his back seat she saw horns. From Crystal's face she could tell she'd seen them too. Wherever they were going, at least some of them were going together.

TRUCKS

The light on the microwave glowed across the bench. 2 a.m. Rollo walked out the back door and down the bank to the highway, pulling on a sweatshirt as he went. He put his toes on the rumble strips on the side of the road and leaned into the updraft of the trucks as they thundered past. They came in huge lines of fury and their rushing engines pulled Rollo another step forward. The air changed direction and shoved him away as they swept past, eddies of spray twisting up into the sky.

After the trucks had gone by Rollo walked down the side of the highway and through the tunnels to the city. There was a little green car parked on the street near the tunnel exit. He looked up at the dark houses and then pushed his steel ruler down the inside of the window and stole it. He scooted the seat forward and drove slowly through town, holding himself up with the steering wheel. He cruised by Jenna's rotting house, his school girlfriend. Sometimes if he pulled up she'd be listening and come outside but this time she didn't.

He turned back to town and rolled slowly through the streets but there was nothing happening except a couple of homeless people shuffling around and picking up cigarette butts. He was just about to ditch the car when a cop pulled in behind him. The cop didn't turn on the siren but his blue and reds were on, revolving lazily. Rollo kept going for a couple more blocks and the cop kept following so he pulled over and shuffled down in his seat with the doors locked. The officer got out and stood by Rollo's door with his hands on his belt. Another cop car pulled up and a policewoman came and stood around as well. She knocked on the window and asked Rollo his name and address but he didn't say anything and they knew who he was anyway. Finally the male cop broke the driver side window and stood there not touching him until Rollo got sick of their friendly voices and got out of the car. He ignored their questions and went and sat in the back of the cruiser.

At his house his parents came out and apologised and said they'd bring him in for court in the morning. After the cop car lights stopped bleeding their blue and red through the curtains and all over the floor Rollo's parents went back to bed with tired faces and blank eyes.

Alone again in the kitchen, the microwave light flashed its constant message at Rollo. Rollo let himself back outside.

The only place open in town was the bakery. "Any buns?" Rollo said into the doorway. The old ladies shook their heads and he stood still with slices of his body visible through the plastic curtain strips until they gave him one. He rode his scooter down the main street as the sun started to come up, clacking slowly over the cobblestones.

Rollo wanted to steal a truck. He wanted to bear down on people like a huge thundering angel. He'd climbed up on a few and looked through the window at the gear sticks when the trucks were parked up in town but sometimes the driver was still in it, sleeping in the cab. The rest of the time Rollo knew they'd be in a hotel nearby, with one ear pricked for kids like him. They were big men. They weren't ladies or cops. They might hit him and throw him on the road, or lock him in the truck with them.

Rollo rode his scooter to Jenna's house to see if she was up yet. When he got close he saw there was a condemned sign on the door and the house was empty. He let himself in a window and wandered through the rooms. He saw where they'd been burning rubbish in the fireplace, and damp holes in the floor. He reached around in some of the holes looking for a bottle of beer or maybe a photo of her, getting dirt under his nails, not really hoping. There was broken glass swept into a corner. Rollo touched the stickers on Jenna's door. She hadn't had time to peel them off.

On the way home Rollo found a truck idling at a gas station. The driver was inside the shop. Rollo didn't even think about it, he climbed up the wheel and into the cab. He put his head down and started pulling and pushing at the gears, kicking at the pedals with his feet. The truck began to roar and then to scream. Rollo was crying too. Then the truck driver was at the door, ripping it open and swearing. He reached in and Rollo stabbed at his hands with his pocket knife but it was small and he had to push hard. Red holes appeared in the driver's hands but he didn't seem to notice so Rollo kicked the passenger door open behind him and tumbled backwards out of the truck, cracking his head on the road. He pulled himself up on the tyre and ran stumbling through the carpark. Rollo knew he was weaving and running in circles with the crack on his head gouting blood and that the driver could catch him, but the driver wasn't following. Rollo stopped and looked back at the truck. The driver was just sitting in the seat with his cab light on, flexing his big hands in front of him and shaking his head.

Rollo walked home with the sounds of flies buzzing in his head and one of his eyelids hanging fatly over his eye. It was turning into a hot sickly morning and the alcoholics were out drinking in their deck chairs. They watched Rollo with their eyes over their beards. One of their dogs sniffed after Rollo's feet and followed him silently, full of promise, for almost a block. When he got to the highway and its barrelling trucks the dog retreated, staring and growling. Rollo imagined it getting run over, being flung into the bushes. But he wasn't mad at the dog.

The house was empty when Rollo opened the front door. He made himself a coffee, reaching up over the laughing microwave clock for the kettle and the sugar. As he sat on the stoop to drink it, it started to rain with fat warm drops. The house next door erupted with male shouting. Rollo put his cup down and crept to the fence and put his eye to the crack. The neighbours were skinheads and even though Rollo was white it would still be stupid to be caught watching. They were jumping around in the rain with a bar of soap and laughing, bubbles running off their prickled heads and down their pudding-like muscles. Rollo went back inside and looked in the mirror. No one except the police had spoken to him in two days. He put on a big jacket.

The same truck was at the same gas station the next night. It was still raining and Rollo was the only one around. The truck wasn't idling but Rollo climbed up on the wheel, cupped his hands to the driver's side window and peered in. He looked back at the station. The driver was sitting low in a booth, hat pulled low on his bald head, rolls of flesh hanging out under it. Rollo opened the cab door and got in. There was a scuffed biscuit tin on the front seat. The truck driver's lunch was inside, stacked sandwiches in grease paper. Rollo ate one as he opened the visor, emptied the coin tray, pulled papers out of the glovebox. The peanut butter was thick and stuck in his mouth. There was a steering lock on the steering wheel this time and no keys but Rollo still pulled the levers back and forth. He stretched his toes down to press the pedals. He looked back at the gas station and the driver was at the counter. He wiped his hands on the seat and hopped out.

Rollo slept at home for the rest of the night. His parents walked back and forth across the doorway, like ghosts. Neither of them stopped to fill the doorway.

The next time it was still unlocked. There were

sandwiches and a tan slice in the tin. The steering lock was still on and the driver still sat side on in the station with his hat pulled low. There was an engine manual on the other seat. Rollo ate a sandwich and leafed through it, pulling the levers back and forth.

MISSING

On Sunday Shane came to visit for family dinner and I was face down on the lawn after eating everything in the medicine cupboard. Instead of telling our parents he draped me over the back fence to puke it out. "Do that again you little shit," he said, "and you better take the rest of us with you." He took me to the doctor and told me what to ask for. "You'll be alright once you get to my age," he said. We went back to the routine family dinners, Shane coming over each Sunday, until he went missing.

It was uncommon, but not impossible. People drank too much and tried to swim the river. Some moved away without telling anyone. Usually everyone found out what happened, but with Shane no one had been with him. No one had seen him.

By the time I was sixteen he'd been gone for nine months. I'd been babysitting at a hotel on the waterfront and when the parents got home and handed me a fistful of coins they were drunk enough not to notice that I only pretended to call a taxi. It was midnight and the lake sucked the light out of the air. Nine months. As long as a baby took to finish growing lungs, fingers.

I wasn't ready to go home. The lake was playing a whispering tune at the shore with cold fingers. A car went past, boys in it shouting and laughing. I stared after it. The car pulled into the lookout ahead and spun in a slow circle, headlights picking out road, dark water, sand. It came back and pulled over on the opposite side of the road, all the windows down.

"Hey, girl!" I kept walking.

"Girl, come here!" They sounded like a car of Shanes. I missed him. I walked over the sand, onto the pavement, and up to the car windows.

"Get in. You wanna ride? We'll take you home. You can't walk at night. Rapists." I looked into the car. It was full of twenty-somethings, the same age as Shane. They did look like him. Smelled like him.

"Do you know Shane?" I asked. I wanted to cry, all of a sudden. The boys looked at each other.

"I did," said one. "Why?"

"He's my brother," I said, refusing to use the past tense as they did.

Five minutes after that I was home. I'd been hoping for something more, some sort of danger, but they were just normal guys. They'd gone searching when he'd gone missing, door knocking, poking sticks into the river. They just dropped me off. One of the boys shut the door behind me and the car pulled away. I felt like Shane was leaving me there all over again. I looked up at my family home. The safety light was on out the front, and nightlights were glowing in the kids' rooms. I just couldn't escape it.

Seventeen. Shane would be twenty-nine. I left school and worked at the pet store and came home to sleep and wash my clothes. Mum had more kids, a boy and a girl, to a nice guy called Richard. They waved at me from the table where they were strapped into high chairs and I forced myself to sit with them, to lean over and cut up their fish fingers. But family tables are scarred fields where you can't escape what someone might say next. Mum caught me as I mashed up my baby sister's pie and sniffed her wispy hair in its little sprout on top of her head. "Hey love," Mum said. "Richard and I were thinking that it might be nice if you had room to park your car in the garage." After the police had let everything sit at Shane's unit for a month they had let me and Mum in to pick it all up and bring it home. There wasn't a lot, a dirt-bike he'd kept in the lounge, a stack of books by the toilet, clothes and some soap. The soap had a hair on it.

"Well, yeah," I said. Knowing what she was asking. Hating myself. "You should've gotten rid of it all ages ago."

Mum's eyes welled with tears. There had been visible rising hope in her face that I might argue for Shane's return, argue that he was alive somewhere and just taking his time. The look on her face was naked and infuriating. My own hope was selfish. I did not want to share it.

"He obviously doesn't fucking want it, Mum." I made the 'Mum' into a rapier, slid it in between the lungs.

"Hey, well, hey now..." started Richard. It was the ridiculousness of his interjection that made me stop. That and his small children sitting in their seats, chins level with the table, big buggy eyes staring at me. Shane, if he was a ghost, stared at me too. The big sister.

I couldn't do it. I packed up my own stuff and moved into a single flat on the other side of town, desperately lonely, with a view of the grey water. I couldn't be near the decisions that would have to happen. What to keep, what to sell. Couldn't watch some young local kid from the window while he passed over money and loaded my brother's dirt-bike from our garage onto his father's truck. Couldn't watch mum watching.

Sometimes when I walked to work I saw the car that had taken me home after babysitting. They waved out to me each time. I thought of Shane's car, which they'd found neatly parked in his driveway. I thought of him as a twenty-something pulling up next to me in his car, walking home from school with my friends, bending the planks of my sandals under my toes with each step for something to do. "Get in shithead," he used to say. "I'll give you a ride home from school."

Eighteen. It would be his thirtieth birthday. To celebrate I drank too much at a party and fell all the way from the top of the outside stairs to the bottom. As I lay there I imagined Shane at parties, hitting on girls. He would have been good at it. He'd been kind. I lay and thought about ditches. Concrete in peoples' backyards with hidden bodies under them. Anywhere that he could be.

A couple of plump white legs walked into view. I could see up the girl's skirt.

"What are you doing?"

"Resting," I said.

The girl squatted down, skirt hanging open. She didn't seem to care, didn't realise the moonlight picked out her skin like crystal.

I sat up. The girl held out a joint that she'd come out with and we sat in the dirt together and smoked. Her name was Margaret. She went back upstairs by herself and then came down with a couple bottles of liquor she'd stolen from someone's cupboard.

We ended up at the lakefront, sitting on the edge of the lookout.

"Your brother's gone."

She knew who I was already. I didn't know what to say. She hadn't said dead, or missing, just gone. He wasn't anything definable, he was just not there anymore. I didn't say anything.

She didn't seem in a hurry to go anywhere. We sat looking out at the lake. Small crests of water jostled up from the depths. Margaret kicked her legs softly. I looked at her. She had a round face, white and balloonish. Short black hair. Her skin was very pale, and her arms and legs were puffed and short. I thought of Snow White, but fatter. When I spoke she looked down and nodded often, as if agreeing with herself. She seemed centred, hard to unbalance. She wore a skirt. Sensible shoes. Red lipstick.

The water pulled back from the shore and came in

again. I felt sober and tired. "I have to go," I said.

"Hold on," Margaret stood up and surveyed me. "Here." She pulled a cheap deodorising spray from her handbag and sprayed me from top to toe with it. Strangely, I felt better.

A month later I watched as Margaret, sweating and grunting, hauled a girl under her. She clamped her with her thighs and pulled the girl's arm up toward her until the girl squeaked. The referee stopped them, and Margaret rolled off, panting. She competed in wrestling and I came along to watch as much as I could because it was weird. It could have been hilarious, but Margaret was in earnest, as she was about everything. She would solemnly show me her latest bout of ringworm from the mats and instead of quitting she just brought her own disinfectant to practise and sprayed it over everything, not caring what anyone thought. I was obsessed with her strangeness. Shane could even be alive in a world so strange.

We spent our weekends together, usually stopping by parties of people we hardly knew. Margaret was striking in her unnatural dumpiness. People looked when we entered a room. Snow White and the dead boy's sister. I scanned every face for my brother. When Margaret got her learner's licence she drove us into the next town the very same day, crunching through the gears. From then we went somewhere new in her car whenever we could, searching.

Shane's friends still went past in their car. They were the same age as my brother would have been, could be. The two tenses were habit whenever I thought of him. Would have been, could still be. Two Shanes. One dead, one alive. Years of this made me feel tired. I found a boyfriend through Margaret's wrestling club and I watched them both at tournaments, rising through the ranks. My boyfriend was calm and strong and his conversations rested easy on me. I started to stay in. Margaret went on longer and longer drives without me and then eventually she just didn't come back. I knew she'd be fine. Nothing could un-centre that gnome.

We moved to the city and lived there nearly long enough to expect to get married. I stopped searching, stopped counting the years of Shane's life. But we ran out of easy things to say or do and he ended it. *We need to break up,* he'd said. Not, *we need a break,* or, *we need to talk.* There was nowhere to go from there. He'd gone back to our hometown. I stayed in the city, not really sure what else to do. Not long later at a bar a woman detached herself from a loud group of business-people after five and followed me into the bathroom. I still lived in the city, killing time. If you'd asked me on the spot I couldn't have told you how old Shane might be.

The woman came in and approached her own reflection. She whispered something to herself in the mirror. She had thick black eyelashes weighing down the top lids. Her reflection smiled, small teeth everywhere. "You shouldn't wear jeans without heels unless you want to look stumpy, Katherine," she said. She stared at me in the mirror. Then with the grab of a purse and a rush of perfumed air she was gone. I followed her out onto the street, a strange fortuitous character in a world that felt strange, unreal. I had missed that feeling.

I wasn't used to seeing her in a pencil skirt. Her muscles ballooned up under it. We had dinner. Margaret said she'd looked for Shane. She wasn't afraid of the subject. She'd followed a group who had claimed to kill a guy but he'd turned out to be someone different and she'd tipped off the police anonymously. She'd let herself into halfway houses, peering at the people sleeping in the dirt. She seemed to want me to know that she'd always looked for Shane — that she, like me, was still willing to believe he was missing. I was grateful for that.

Of course he was in the lake. When they did find him I'd been fifteen years without him. Margaret and I had a small unit with soft white furniture and cross stitch on the walls. I thought she might ask me to marry her soon. I'd say yes. She was still a wrestler. Absurd. Impossible to lose.

The police had been looking for a teenage couple who had gone missing near the cliffs and they'd sent divers into the lake. No one had thought to go into the water for Shane when he'd disappeared because he'd lived on the other side of town and his car had been at home. The walk would have been so long and so cold. They'd found the teenagers hiding in a garage at one of their friend's houses. I fantasised about making a swap, putting the teenagers in the lake to find Shane alive in a garage with a girlfriend. Mostly though, I stared at Margaret, unwilling to comprehend. I was stunned by the proof of it. *If you do that again you better take the rest of us with you.* The phone rang. It was my sister, no longer a chubby baby but a girl smarter than anyone about the emotions of the adults around her. Yes, I would come home for a funeral of sorts. Yes, I'd bring Margaret. I thought about Shane's walk, bundled up against the cold. After I hung up I looked up Shane's old address, packed a warm scarf for the lake air. Margaret looked at my suitcase and put in her scarf too.

SANDWICHES

Tulip was laughing silently at her tiny sandwich. She'd picked it up by the margarine side. Betty tried her hardest not to look. Tulip didn't know what to do with the margarine on her finger because they were in a conference about selling comprehensive travel insurance for exotic places and really, Tulip and Betty should not have been sitting next to each other because they got like this. Tulip held her finger up to Betty in a state of anxiety and Betty took a big snorting breath in an effort not to laugh and they both began to whimper. The speaker paused. Everyone turned around and looked at them. Betty and Tulip stood abruptly and their mother hissed "naughty girls," and they walked the agonising ten metres to the door with their heads down and moaning giggles slipping out on their way. Betty was dizzy with horror and Tulip put her sandwich down on the table as they left and the girls knew they would not be getting this travel opportunity or any other until they could control themselves.

Another room of people, another table of tiny sandwiches. They knew they shouldn't sit together but there were two seats reserved for them at the front, of course there were. The coffin looked short, like she'd been cut in half by age. It was their turn to speak. Tulip was shaking and Betty held her hand and they stumbled over their words together both praying, *don'tfuckitupdon'tfuckitupdon'tfuckitup*. Their own children were there and their husbands were holding their babies and *oh god they couldn't laugh, not at the kids' grandma's funeral* and their grips on each other's hands grew tighter.

After the service everyone else wanted to thaw out and chuckle but Tulip and Betty were finally stony faced. They didn't want a cup of tea, they didn't want a sausage roll or even a glass of wine. They stared at the table of tiny sandwiches and wondered how they could ever have thought they were so funny.

The minister entered and gave them a small nod and they both got up and followed him while everyone else in the room took care not to watch. The girls had a last goodbye, just the two of them, stroking the shiny wood of the casket and whispering. They looked at the minister and he pressed a discreet button hidden in the wall. The coffin began to trundle down the conveyor to the incinerator but it was so stumpy and light that it rattled from side to side like a shitty little train and Betty whispered "oh noo," and Tulip convulsed and they rested their heads on each other's shoulders and the minister stepped out of the room.

WINTER

(Previously published in Mindfood)

Sarah watched a fruit fly drift past her head and reached for it. It moved around her hand opening and closing on the air in an unfair comparison of proportion and dipped into the saucepan she'd been eating out of. She knew she should rinse the pot but she just moved her gaze away. Above her, a pale painting of a lady with a crooked neck watched the apricots leaning against each other in the fruit bowl. The two of them sat together in silence. Sarah's eyes were grainy and sore. Every morning they burned and itched with allergies from cat hair and dust because she couldn't bring herself to clean so she just sat and rubbed at them tiredly. She imagined what she must look like, a blister eyed creature in a dressing gown, greasy hair folding over itself, feet hard and cold against the kitchen floor. She felt her skin was going grey.

George had given her a kiss on his way out the door, not asking why she was sitting in the kitchen on his office chair that belonged in the spare room. A perfunctory morning kiss that said *hello,* and, *I'm glad you're here, but I have to go to work — are you going to do something today?* He had stroked her hair absently, noting the greasy feel (she imagined) and had closed the door softly behind him, as if Sarah were still asleep.

She had thought at first when she had dragged the chair into the kitchen that she might do the dishes. But staring at them now she knew that she would just upset the pile and she just couldn't go through with it. Perhaps when the sun climbed further and they didn't gleam so dully at her.

By now George would be in the city at his computer, planning with pipes and paths on a screen, mapping a future for somebody in concrete and steel. His faith was absurdly innocent to Sarah. *In five years, this will all be here.* She imagined him on the bus every morning, briefcase settled on his lap or perhaps held tightly against his chest if it was crowded, his stubble scraping across the canvas every time he moved. She wondered if he talked to people, if he had people he nodded to that took the same bus every day. Sarah didn't have anywhere to be so she took different buses and recognised no-one.

She was still staring at the sink. The neighbour walked past and looked curiously in the window, so she ducked her head and picked up a dish cloth. When he was gone she put it down again. She kept her muscles rigid, so as not to let the cold into the relaxed spaces.

She wanted to do something today. She needed to go to the bank, needed to vacuum and bake something and make the house warm and inviting. She felt like communicating with someone, reasserting her personality in the world before it faded away forever. She could visit friends, but didn't want to. The phone looked cold and uninviting. A letter, then. She felt ready to write one — but what would she write? And to who? She wanted to write to her sister. They had kept in touch vaguely but Sarah hadn't really known her in years. Didn't know what made her laugh, what interested her — they used to repeat lines from funny movies they had watched together. How sad to write the same old jokes. As if she hadn't progressed either. No. Better not to look back. A chatty letter, one that was friendly but dry and not too involved. She could tell her what she'd been up to. And what was that? *Dear Chrissie, this morning I sat in my kitchen and looked at the dishes and thought about what my husband saw in me. I decided not to go to the bank but I did eventually have a shower and put on some undemanding clothes. How about you? Has everything stopped? Do you feel as if your skin has turned grey?*

She put the paper down, unmarked. She decided to shower first so that her letter would not be a lie before she even wrote it, a catalyst of exaggerations.

There was a dead moth in the bottom of the shower. If she had been in the bathroom first, while it was slumping and staggering and beating itself in circles, she would have stopped the water and put it on the windowsill to dry itself out. She hated the feel of their fat, soggy bodies, but hated more the feeling of responsibility that she wished had never occurred to her. She knew they didn't know anything about her, wouldn't know the difference, but considered the rescues little sacrifices of her own that would add up one day.

When she and George were together it was different. She let him direct the water at the bugs, flush them down the drain. It never occurred to him to feel responsible and she didn't feel the same guilt when he was there. This one was dead anyway. Sarah turned on the water and bowed her head, watched the little body tear apart.

Not long after they had married, they had sat inside at the window with the lights on and watched the bugs outside crawling urgently along the glass, the reflection of the light bulb floating in the sky. She thought of the moths now as George had pointed out to her then, fluttering and bumping into each other. Not mating, feeding, or even fighting; just concentrating so hard on the lights inside that they had become irrelevant to one another, unrecognisable as members of the same species. She remembered his kiss bumping against her forehead on his way out the door and held her arms tight to her chest, so that the water pooled up against her.

She told George about the moths, after going to the bank and looking in a bookstore, after they caught the bus home from the city together in silence. He kissed her again, on the mouth, and said she had a big imagination. She cycled through feeling hurt at this to feeling loved and then, as always, melancholy because of it. *Does he know I'm a black hole and there's nothing there?* She thought. And then directly on the tail of that: *he knows, and he's trying to gloss it over.* And after that: *he knows, and he doesn't mind, and he wants me not to mind.* So Sarah tried not to mind.

The dishes were still heaped on top of one another when they got home so George poured a glass of wine and filled the sink. He made it hot and bubbly, like he'd run her a bath. She started scrubbing and the dried food just slipped away. He let her keep her hands in the water while he dried. Sarah didn't like to dry because it was like putting dirt back onto everything. After another glass of wine she said she was sorry for being so much work and George said she thought too much of herself. Sarah smiled and, absurdly, welled up with tears. She pushed his arm so it skidded along the pot he'd been holding, so that he wouldn't notice.

They'd eaten on the way home but the dishes were done and the kitchen was theirs so they had another glass of wine, standing steadily on the brown linoleum and looking at each other. He asked what she had done today and she said, not much. She shrugged and smiled as she said it, an effort to let him know she wouldn't be like this always.

"Shall we go into the city and look at the divers?" he said. It brought back the memory, and they wouldn't go because going wouldn't compare, but it showed he was still trying with her. They had been drinking wine, like tonight, finishing a bottle from the neck at the bus stop.

The bus was so late but when it came they thanked the driver anyway, got on, smiling goodwill at everybody and rolling slightly when the engine started. She had been quiet on the bus but he had known by then that she liked to feel each movement, watch the condensation and warm her back on the brightly coloured seats. He hadn't believed her at first when she said she loved buses, travelling, even the soggy trip into the city, but to see her then, smiling slightly at each stop, he would believe anything.

They were going to go out to meet friends and dance, but they had been late and their friends had gotten cold and sober and gone home. So the two of them had gone to a strip club instead, drawn in like curious insects by the pink light pulsing out the door and onto the street. Inside it was smokey and dim, blurring the edges of skin until everything looked soft and perfect. Loud drunk voices coming in were soon lulled into murmuring, watching the stage in a rolling cabin of liquor and shell-pink light. They had ordered drinks and then they had watched the mermaids. When someone dropped money into a pool, a dancer would swim to get it. When they had first heard of it they had thought it would be beautiful, soft pink mermaids in a pool, turning like elegant fish. But here was one now, hair straggling across big yellow goggles, bubbles streaming from her nose. The tank was tall so that she had to kick to keep upright, splaying her legs awkwardly, bunting the glass and bobbing around. They looked at her like she was in an aquarium and she blinked out at them and the image provided a backdrop of hilarity that could be conjured at any moment, an inexhaustible sign that things could not be so serious. They had run out of money and wandered home, Sarah clutching George's sleeves to stop spinning in the headlights of waiting taxis.

Different then to tonight; where they did not go out but thought about that one time, had another glass of wine and watched TV. The bottle sat swaddled in a blanket between them. The curtains were closed against the moths fluttering fatly outside. They grew social and invited around friends but it was too late, everyone had set their alarms and planned for sleep. Sarah became tired and went to bed. George stayed up with a bottle of Merlot and his computer and crawled in next to her sometime in the morning. They rested against each other like tired travellers, forehead to forehead until Sarah woke and felt condensation from his breath on her lips. She couldn't think how to thank him for marrying her and so she got up, put on a load of washing and put the empty bottles in the recycling bin. Today she would write to her sister. She would write about their trip to the city, pretend it was last night instead of years ago, would ask how her sister had been doing.

She found a blank page, discarded her pen after the indent would not fill with ink, picked another from the drawer and wrote, her fingers cold, stumbling over themselves:

Eggs
Bread
Tomato sauce

Avocado
Apricots x4
Crossed out the *x4* and replaced it with *x2*. Last time they had gone soft.

TULIPS

On the road ahead of Claire were two boys she recognised dragging —dogs? —no, goats — backwards across the asphalt. They were brothers. They were also her students, truant from the last class of the day. One of them was on the centre line with his jaw clamped down and his arm around the goat's chest, waiting for a gap in traffic. The other was already over the road, holding his goat by a back leg. They stared at Claire as she drove slowly through the tableau and she smiled at them, even though she knew they probably both hated her.

Claire continued driving up the hill. She lived an hour over the other side of a small mountain, descending into fog each morning to teach at the local school and then rising out of it in the afternoons, crawling behind the logging trucks. The town where she taught was supposed to be quaint, that's what the website said, but it didn't mention the lack of light in the main street, the saggy houses behind the railway line. There was a job advertised to manage the train station. Every week it was re-advertised while the sign out front lost paint in flakes.

Claire drove slowly up the bends, thinking about work. The sun cut in and out, blocked off by damp native trees. One of the students had called her stupid today. It was more often *bitch*, which she liked better, because on the days she was a bitch she wasn't quite prey. She looked down and realised she'd only been travelling 80kmph. Guiltily, she pressed down on the accelerator and lifted a hand to the ute behind her. *Sorry*. But the ute, already behind this slow car too long, powered past her on a blind corner and up into the hills, the dogs on the back skittering across the tray and barking.

At home, to avoid her panic attack, Claire replanted the flowers that had been dying in pots outside. She dug a little hole in the ground with her trowel and grasped each plant by the thickest part, just above the roots. She crumbled the sides of the roots so they would grow. She planted them, pressed the dirt down, hands certain.

Claire lived alone. She chose cheap houses on the back of farms in order to pay the whole rent, where the farmers learned quickly about her soft nature and dropped off mis-mothered lambs by the handful for her to rear. Her family thought it was sad to live up a gravel driveway so far away from anything but Claire was grateful to do it all herself. She wouldn't be left by anyone she had relied on, not like her mother who was left standing in the driveway, with nothing but dirty hands and saggy blouses and *can garden* on her résumé. So Claire paid her cheap rent and worked a job she wasn't good at and hoped people there would like her enough to keep her from being lonely. Claire shook her head. She wasn't going to think like that. Thoughts like that left fractures. She *liked* her lambs and her students. They were just making her more resilient.

Morning. Claire ate her porridge gazing out over the paddocks, the lights of the quadbikes criss-crossing as the shepherds moved the first mobs of sheep in the dark. She got in her car and drove back to work, an hour over the hill. As Claire drove, her mind churned over the day ahead, the day behind. There was a spot on her chin that she must not touch. Her hand kept straying to it. It was raining. A car turned its lights off as it went past. Had it just turned its lights off? Or had it flashed its lights? Was there something on the road ahead? She slowed down, saw a car behind her, didn't want to seem too slow, sped back up again.

At school one of the teachers in the staffroom said her name. Claire looked up, smiling, but the teacher was talking to the principal. "Well those students outside yesterday, they were Claire's. And I told them to be quiet, I had a test going on. And they wouldn't." Claire went to the bathroom. The principal met her eye as she slid past.

Claire walked down the mustard hallway hunched deep into her ski jacket. The students ignored her, streaming around her and pushing their earphones in deeper when she tried to talk to them. One rolled a smoke as he walked. "What are you doing?" she asked.

"Fuck off," he said.

There was a message on her personal cell phone after the first period. A parent. Angry. Her son was not progressing. He needed to get his credits so he could move out and get a job. What was Claire doing about it?

Third period. Global studies. The students were hot and argumentative. "Why do we have to learn this? What has this got to do with anything?" Claire began to patiently explain. But they were already sick of her. They began to concentrate on each other.

"Sieg," one called out.

"Yoza," shouted another.

The girls sat on their phones and waited for the day to be over. A boy made lines out of a paracetamol on his desk and snuffed them up his nose. "Why do you dress like that?" a student asked her.

The end of lunch. Claire waited for her last class to arrive. She arranged her folders, trying not to look vulnerable as they came in. Outside a fight started. The one who started it was the quick loser. He burrowed his face down into the other boy's chest, to limit the punches only to the back of his head. "Go and get someone!" shouted Claire, knowing no one would. She went for the door, wondering what she was going to do when she got there.

But it was already over. A large senior who barely spoke but nodded at Claire when she sat next to him in class had pulled them apart. He held them, one polo shirt in each fist. The senior shrugged his shoulders at Claire. What would she like him to do with them?

At home the lambs wailed incessantly until they were fed. It was raining so hard that Claire sobbed as she fed them, so cold, so uncomfortable, angry that they took her for granted, that they were right, she would never let them just starve. That she'd never just tell them to *fuck off.*

Saturday morning. Sunny. The tulips weren't coming up where Claire had planted them. The shoots grew in haphazard clumps, as if they'd wormed toward each other under the soil, in secret. She couldn't control anything. Claire lay down on her stomach and counted them, raking the surface softly with her fingertips. Sturdy and sleek they had shoved the crust of dirt aside overnight, leaving deep cracks.

She heard the crunch of gravel and leaped up, heart pounding. How long had she been there? She was lying on the *grass*, for goodness' sake. But it was just one of the rams on the driveway, who had also gotten a fright and was staring at her with his chin raised. Claire went inside. 2 p.m. She dialled home.

"What's that? I can't hear over—"

Claire switched off the kettle, poured the water half warmed into her tea cup.

"Hi Mum."

"That's better. I saw a house advertised around the corner, Vic and Bill's old—

"With the cat?"

"No, with the green roof — anyway it's *really* cosy, Vic and Bill were old so you know it'll be warm and—"

"Mum I can't really afford—"

"and you could teach young children rather than —"

"It's a different degree mum—" Claire didn't mention she was afraid of the parents of small children.

"Did you see on the news, a PE teacher had his collarbone *broken* by a teenage—"

"It was rugby—"

"And they have the sweetest little garden—"

"Did I tell you my tulips are coming up?"

"Oh no, it's too early for those where you are, *much* too cold —isolated — they'll be up a bit la—"

"I'd better go mum, I've got some marking to do. I'll send you a picture of the garden."

"Love you Bub."

"Love you."

Claire got up, stoked the fire, picked up cups and put them on the bench. Some babies are born into duty as clearly as if it has been inked on their foreheads in their mother's blood. The duty is whispered again into their tiny seashell ears by their fathers. Claire knew eventually she would leave her house and her job which wasn't proving anything to anybody, go home to her duty. She wasn't even any good at her job anyway.

To ease the tightness in her chest Claire spent some time on her computer looking at luxury hotels. The hotel rooms were bright and airy. They had clean linen and slick tiles where thoughts just slid right off. The chair in the corner was impersonal. The desk was the same in every room. She looked around her own living room where her thoughts had been wearing down the corners, wearing down the furniture, the walls, the door. She began to breathe faster. She put the jug on and closed the curtains against the hundreds of sheep eyes in the dark.

After her panic attack and while she was wringing out her cold flannel Claire thought she might buy a cyclamen flower for the laundry. She looked at them online. Shocking pinks. She would place hers on the shelf above the washing machine. But the water from the tub beside the washing machine had been splashing back, running down the side between the whiteware. She had been thinking about this for a while now, how it would need to be pulled out and wiped. Then she remembered there were spots of mould on the ceiling of the bathroom and she had to change the sheets in the spare room. She felt like putting something over her head and crying. But easier than crying was getting a sponge and wiping one thing at a time.

Claire had a dream. In it she was rummaging through dirt with her hands, looking for her bulbs. She pulled them up, held them, secure in their weight. She replanted them, pressing them down. Then she frantically scrabbled back through the dirt, breaking the crust with her nails, pulled them back up, checked they were still there.

School again. Who cares which day now. Claire looked at the posters on the back wall as she talked about apostrophes. Two of the posters had fallen halfway down. There was a rumble, a stock truck going by. The students stopped their chatting to listen. Ignore it, Claire was about to say. Do your work. But the rumble got louder. The desks began to hum. An earthquake, then. Claire waited to see what it would do. She didn't want to begin the battle of getting them under their desks. The rumble increased and the desks began to jitter. *No... Hold...* She thought to herself. The books tumbled off the bookshelf. The floor began to roll. The students watched her. Her mother and her lambs waited for her. Was she going to say anything? The rumble became a roar. *Is there even enough room under my desk?* Claire thought. The floor bucked. Time to get under cover. There was a deep groan and everyone looked up. All Claire's thoughts slipped off the deeply-grooved tracks. She could just stop worrying now. She clicked her throat to speak her first entirely natural word, and the first thin cracks sprinted across the ceiling.

TESSA ANN

Tessa Ann grew up in a house with guinea pigs living under the floor. At night the children lay in their beds and listened to them scutter. Someone, one of her mother's sisters, or even one of her grandmother's sisters, had owned a pair and they had gotten out. Instead of dying in the frost they'd multiplied. When Tessa Ann's mother had her morning coffee and cigarette on the front steps in the sun, surrounded by children, their fat sleek bodies trundled out from under the porch and across the lawn. The fur was long and glossy. It reached to the grass.

Marlene was her mother's name. Marlene's mother before her had been psychic and they all had dreams about her where she smiled at them reassuringly. The older dead men in Tessa Ann's family were distant. Their ghosts didn't talk and no one called on them.

Marlene's children went crazy in cycles. Tessa Ann's hairdresser told her that hair had a seven-year cycle. Your hair could be curly for seven years, then straight. Blonde, then brown. The crazy of Tessa Ann's siblings was like that. They used routines to put their lives into manageable boxes. But when the routines got too manic it would mean they were about to blow wide open. Some of them never slept. Some of them sat and stared. They took turns and helped each other. They made do.

When Tessa Ann grew older and it was her turn to feel like stopping showering and stopping eating and crawling under the house with the guinea pigs, she thought of her psychic grandmother's bedroom at the back of the house where they'd grown up. It had been cream and green and from it you could hear the whole house as if underwater. While Marlene had corralled her siblings in the front rooms Tessa Ann had lifted her grandmother's perfume. She'd touched the sea shells.

Their father was calm. They got some of his blood to soften the ghosts and most of Tessa Ann's siblings when they grew up could keep jobs. Some of them even paid their bills. Tessa Ann remembered the mess when they were young, the children all running around underfoot and screaming every morning. *What if I can't find my homework? What if there's an earthquake? What if our parents die and we all have to live alone? What if a man with a bat stands in the front yard we have to choose who dies?*

Their father had pinned a page written in yellow highlighter to the hallway wall. It had a title. They crowded around it. The title said, "The Getting Ready Chart." On it were pictures he'd drawn. A picture of a hairbrush, pulling through long, flowing hair. A picture of shoes, with laces tied. A picture of a toothbrush, with impossibly large teeth. "Brush your teeth," it said. "Brush your hair," it said. "Get your shoes ready," it said.

Tessa Ann and her siblings still thought of the chart when they were grown. On those days when they could hear the guinea pigs scratching in their dreams and the cats getting under the house to kill them and they woke up crazy in spite of themselves, they counted their hours of sleep, set alarms, woke up and brushed their hair, they brushed their teeth, they found their clothes and they put them on and they did not crawl under the house. They got out the door and went to school and when they grew up they went to work.

When the children left home Marlene had gifts for all of them. *This one is rose quartz. For your heart. This one is moonstone. To protect you from demons. This is a knife. Put it in your boot. Don't sit in rooms with men without one there to protect you. This is a dream catcher. It lets the bad ones fall through. This is my phone number. For if anyone has come to get you.*

Tessa Ann got a nice boyfriend who looked out for her for many years. He was kind to her. He fell in love easily and he sometimes slept with other girls, but he was always sorry and came home and told her and cried because he was so romantic. Eventually her selfish routines and rising panic got too much for him and he left her. Tessa Ann was sad, but she had jobs to do. He didn't like to touch the rubbish, so Tessa Ann did it. He was afraid of the whipping blades on the lawn mower, so Tessa Ann did it. He worried about things like never making enough money and disappointing his parents. Tessa Ann's fears were visceral like being beaten to death by a stranger in the supermarket, they weren't like his. Her parents loved all their children hard, like survivors did.

Marlene had always impressed on them the importance of rich men. Tessa Ann thought that with a rich man she wouldn't have to mow lawns or climb on the roof and pull the muck out of the gutters or carry a knife, so she found one. This man drank nice wines and had a nice kitchen and a cleaner once a week. He took her to dinner. He took her to meet his family, at a rich barbecue at the top of the only three story building in town.

Tessa Ann was careful not to speak at the barbecue because she knew her voice came out as a question, that she laughed at the wrong sort of jokes. The women asked her to come and sit with them, but Tessa Ann could smell danger amidst the nail polish and went to sit with the men in the pool room. You won't believe this, but the mayor was there. Tessa Ann met the mayor. He brought his own bottle of rum in a crystal bottle and drank it all and started reaching for her with red sweaty blooms in his fat cheeks. He did not bother to edit himself in front of Tessa Ann. She kept out of his reach and watched him stumble and slur but he didn't care because she was probably stupid or not even real. Her rich boyfriend drank beer after beer and didn't notice the mayor except to try and get a taste of the rum in the crystal bottle.

Tessa Ann realised she didn't fit and she went

home and never went back to rich men, not even when they asked. They were their worst selves in front of her, and they could not protect her.

The first time Tessa Ann visited her last boyfriend who became her husband she drove herself up his gravel driveway into the heart of a farm. She passed a tractor and a little slaughterhouse. The bucket of the tractor was full of pink guts and red soup. The slaughterhouse was dark and the hooks were swinging.

Tessa Ann's new husband could leap a fence and grab a ewe by the scruff, his other hand tumbling a tangled lamb out of it and onto the ground for it to stand up, gasping. He could hold a bleating ram with his knees and lift its chin with a cupped hand, slit its throat with the other, and let the blood gout out over his knuckles. He was so casually involved with life and with death. He mowed his own lawns and he didn't wear any sunblock — which even Tessa Ann thought was a bit careless. She learned from him and his friends that men fighting were generally unfit. They grew tired before they could really hurt each other. Fists on faces really only caused lumps and thick lips, not much more.

"Look at this," her husband would say, in the beginning. "They're chopping off his arms with a machete." He would thrust his phone at her. "Look at this one, they're burning him alive." He thought the best thing for fear was exposure.

"Stop," she would say, tears running down her cheeks. "I'll see it forever."

On her worst days she fixated on the end of the

world. She told him about how it would go, the lack of resources, the violence, always ending in the men coming into the house. He stopped showing her the videos and instead got her a silent dog which followed around the house at her heels. He buried one of his guns for them in the woods at the back of the farm and gave her a map for how to get there. Tessa Ann never knew if he believed her or if he did it to make her feel better but it worked anyway. Rich men wouldn't do that, men who trusted in the order of things and thought Tessa Ann and all her family were crazy.

You also need to protect yourself, her husband said to her. The first time she was hit, hard, she relaxed completely. It was nowhere near as bad as she had imagined. It was bearable. She signed up for more and more classes. She was not a graceful athlete. Her stride jolted up and down, not quick or smooth at all. The teacher made fun of her, bouncing on his feet and springing out his elbows, protruding his teeth like an idiot. Like she was poor and inelegant. That was what she looked like, he said.

The ridicule was another terrible thing that, after all, was bearable. Five times a week she was ridiculed and hit. The flimsy armour she wore did nothing to deaden the deep silence in her ears after a strike to the top of the head. The arm guards slapped against her arms when they were struck and left grey bruises in lines. Her fingers blistered, peeled, blistered harder. When the men struck her *doh,* her shiny plastic chest cover, her breasts flattened.

She never won a single match, but she felt better

anyway. She drove home over the gravel in the dark, with her sticks across the back seat.

One of her husband's friends pissed off a man called Sal. Tessa Ann did not know what Sal was short for, but her mind always corrected it to *Sally.* He was middle aged, old enough not to be so violent but violent anyway, that strange group she always feared most.

Sal wore track pants. He rode a motorbike and had a stiff leg from an old accident. Even an imagined name like Sally only made him more frightening in its strangeness. He walked into Tessa Ann's property at one of their barbecues and knocked one of her husband's friends down. He put his foot on the younger man's throat. The boy was squirming with his shirt tangled and riding up his belly, like a wriggling white whale. Sal stomped on his face a couple of times, sometimes missing as the guy squirmed, sometimes mashing his foot into the guy's lips, getting dirt in his mouth. The guy kept trying to talk, his voice muffled against Sal's boot.

Here was the man coming into the house. Here he was ruining all her nice friends and soon he would ruin everything. Tessa Ann did not know what to do except watch. She imagined herself standing there with the gun, shooting Sal in his stomach, watching the guts come out. But the gun was out in the woods, in their secret meeting place for the end of the world.

Eventually the proper routine took over. The old man got tired. The boy pulled himself up on the side of a truck and pushed the old man over, pummelled his face a bit. They both got up, leaning on things to catch their breath. The old man got on his motorbike and rode away. "Don't take it personally," said someone, clapping the young man on the shoulder. "He's having a bit of trouble with his wife," he said, in explanation. Tessa Ann let out her breath.

Afterwards, a couple weeks afterwards, after another bout of crazy where she stuck to her routines so hard that she muttered vicious words to herself in the mornings when the clean dishes touched the dirty ones and the side bench was smeared with crumbs and blood and she even once threw her wedding ring on the floor, Tessa Ann's husband came home after he'd been out drinking beer and he stormed into the kitchen and picked her up, laughing. He swung her around, lifting her legs, and Tessa Ann's dead psychic grandmother crowded in close to watch as he stamped Tessa Ann's feet up and down on the dog. The dog barked in excitement and nipped at her legs with his wide open mouth, swallowing up her bare feet. "Watch out for the Sally stomp! Sally stomp!" her husband shouted, while Tessa Ann laughed.

MOUNTAINS

They call this mountain the Mother. The guide tells them the Scandinavian story about how in the beginning the earth and the sea mated and all the people and the animals came pouring out onto the earth in a flurry of foam while the sea rushed away back to his deep. The mountain they call the mother lies with her hips and her breasts facing upwards in large mounds and her face turned toward the sky. The group take their last look up and begin to climb. Paige walks through the summer grass, sweating and heavy behind her tall friends. One of them smokes a cigarette as he walks. When they get to the tree line the cool dirt helps the hot arches in Paige's feet to relax. Seeds trickle down from the treetops and stick to her salted skin.

Near the top there is a narrow pass. They squeeze through in single file, their bags scraping the clay on each side. Paige pushes her stomach slowly through. Out the other side is a little piece of grass and her friends drink a bottle of wine there and they all have cheese. Their packs are lighter for the last little walk up, which is colder and emptier. Looking down from the top Paige imagines the lines of her life spun out on the ground beneath them between this mountain and others far away. She imagines the mother has eyes that cast downwards and follow those fault lines. From up there, perhaps, the mother could have seen Paige celebrate her birthday by herself on the ground, watching a wasp dip into a cloud of midges and kill them one by one. She might have seen Paige's friends come and pick her up and take her for easy walks like a sad little dog. She would have seen Paige in the bath, watching the growing hump emerge. Or watched her wake up from dreams of things like organising and gardening at his house and him always saying *I've realised I love you after all. Come back.* But even mothers couldn't grant dreams. Was the earth afraid? Paige wondered. When all the life burst out over her thighs and the sea rushed away so suddenly?

At home in her little unit Paige cooks a small piece of venison and salts it with the dried juniper and birch she snagged from the mother's passing trees. In the hospital her hands still smell of juniper and she holds them to her face as she breathes. When he comes out of her it is with a rush of blood and a shocking tangle of black hair. The waiting room is empty but the earth moves as the mother turns to look.

TEENAGERS

Kate stood at the top of the hill on the first crumbled step and watched the house through the kitchen window. There were no curtains and all the lights were blazing. Someone was making peanut butter and baked beans on toast, spreading the baked beans cold from the tin. He was taller than the refrigerator. There was a crusted cake tin on the bench.

By the time she got down to the door it was already open. "Liam," the person from the kitchen said.

"Is Hailey here?" Asked Kate.

"Nah. She's moving out. You can choose your room though."

Kate let go of her suitcase. She had travelled six hours on the bus and Hailey was the only person she knew in the city. She thought about saying she'd changed her mind. It was night but the sky was still glowing around them with halos of activity, everywhere lights were on. Not like the pitch black of her town, the people hidden in their beds from 8 p.m. onward, the lake that turned into a deep hole in the dark.

She bumped her suitcase over the cracked door frame. She met Brett, the other flatmate, in the lounge. Brett was fit and thin with a loud voice. He studied politics. The fireplace was boarded over and they all stared at it while they had new flatmate beers. One couch was pink splitted leather and the other was green felt. The cold settled over them. The walls were wet and the wood swelled in its joints.

"This is the house depression built," Liam said, and laughed.

Hailey arrived not long after, carrying a box of tea to welcome Kate. Yes, she had left the house. Liam and she had had a thing and now it was over. She was off home now, bye. She didn't come back.

The next morning Kate cleaned the kitchen, soaked and washed the cake tin. She took the small room so that with her things pressing in around her she would feel warm. She plugged in a lava lamp, put up pictures. Her parents came down with a trailer and moved in a small single bunk bed and a set of drawers. Her mother hung a heavy yellow PVC raincoat on the back of the door. "Your umbrella will break," she said. "You're in the city now." As if thick yellow plastic could keep the city out, keep the person in.

The house was tall and cold. The white walls grew unfairly against the flatmates' thin furniture and each room was an ocean with a lonely bed, an island in the centre. After her bills each week Kate had twenty dollars left. She ate noodles, toast, eggs, cheese. They kept their rubbish stacked outside because they couldn't afford the collection and they drove their cars around with cardboard windows where the glass had been punched out.

There were always at least four people living at the house but the only constants were she, Liam with the peace tattoo waiting to join the army, and Brett who ate tins of tuna and watched the Young and the Restless. The high walls pushed them all together and they became friends. In the mornings they climbed into each other's beds, for someone to talk to. They pulled up the damp sheets and huddled in ridiculous groups of three or four, staring at the door for someone, something to arrive.

At times the population of the house grew to five or six, people sharing beds, dating or not, others sleeping on the couches. Friends passing through for a couple months, taking painting jobs, anyone they could convince to stay and help with rent for a while.

They had no jobs, no friends' houses to go around to, no money to go anywhere else. It was the freest Kate would ever be. She could drink on Tuesdays, or start at 2 a.m. after anyone got home from a night shift, drinking through the morning. She could sleep ten hour nights, take additional naps when she was lonely. With two toilet breaks she could watch three movies in a day, mark it off on the calendar at the end.

Sometimes, when everyone was out and Kate started to worry about her future, not knowing what to do or with who or how, she would wander through her flatmates' rooms, looking for ideas or just for the sun. When she could find sunlight she would curl on their beds or the floor until it was gone. When she couldn't she would go back to her bed and stay there.

The pile of black rubbish bags grew out the front and they walked past them, picking around the maggots that spilled over onto the concrete. There was a mouse in the kitchen that sprinted back and forth between the pantry and the sink but it was so skinny Kate couldn't bear to make it leave.

They flatted with a stranger for a while. His name was Dil, he didn't like to be called Dylan. Kate hated calling him Dil. He wanted to be an actor in the theatre. He was pale and ignored his girlfriend and spiked his albino hair. They hated him. They ate his food, smearing the sauces back up the sides of his leftover containers so they would look full. They stole his bedroom light when the one in the kitchen blew, and he got home after his night shift and woke the whole house up roaring. He got into rages and stuttered and his face flushed deep red. He slept with a sledgehammer against his door as a warning to them, he was Theatrical. He was all they ever talked about. They would have house meetings about him. They laughed about him on the bus. They called him Dilbert or Dilworth. One night they stole his sledgehammer and he ran at Liam with his skinny fists up while they all doubled over laughing and then he left. They missed him. Without Dil they would have hated each other.

They added more flatmates. Jake lived on their green couch for over a month, sleeping on his back with sleep apnea, snarling and choking through the night. He took supplements and vitamins, sprinkled them on his toast and scooped them into his drinks by the tablespoon. He was a bodybuilder but each night his snores told a story of an endless struggle for breath. When they drank he would pick Kate up and shake her like a puppy with a rag doll.

The house was never clean. Kate cleaned the bathroom but at the end of an hour it looked exactly the same as when she started. She sat there with her cleaning sprays and her cloth and scrubbed so hard she scraped off all the paint in the bottom of the tub and forever afterwards there was a metallic stain.

Their hot water got shut off because no one paid for it. Brett ran to and from his political lectures instead of taking the bus, to save money for Friday nights. He'd leave in the mornings and run from their side of the mountain through the tunnel, across the city basin. Eventually he just stopped going to class. He spent his time at home going back and forth between the kitchen and bathroom, holding the boiling kettle, to make a bath an inch deep. Endlessly he went back and forth past the couches until they just wanted to tell him to quit. But he refused to be like them, to splash cold water from the tap onto himself each day as they did, shaking and stuttering and hating the morning.

One evening the boys got drunk and played egg toss on the outside steps, throwing eggs back and forth as they stepped backwards over the broken hunks of concrete. Kate stood and watched, filling her cup from a cask of wine. An hour later Liam and Brett stood at the kitchen door laughing as Kate walked unevenly to the pantry and threw her only egg as hard as she could at the kitchen floor. She could do whatever she wanted.

No one would care, no one would whinge about the egg being there or being gone in the morning. The only person it affected was her and she didn't care, didn't care, didn't care. She covered it with a yellow plastic bag and went to bed.

Winter came, even though it was already cold, even though summer had never really touched the house. They were sick all the time. Kate started having terrors of never being able to breathe again, drowning, watching earth and sky slam themselves together at the horizon again and again. But she didn't go home. They all had self indulgent bouts of sadness that they pointed out in each other. Every night they sat as the cold layered over them and complained, coughed, laughed at each other and their complaints and their coughing.

Sometimes one of them would bring home a cask of wine and they'd pull all their lamps and lights from their bedrooms into the lounge and play Michael Jackson. They'd sing and dance on the ripped chairs with the windows flung open. They danced alone, together, over lava lamps, on the ripped sofas, down the hall. They didn't care. Kate sat outside and smoked, feeling warm. In real life smoking would make her feel sick but this wasn't real life, this was something different. This was the last night. You only had to slash open the windows, lean out over the blazing city lights with drink in hand to know that some things were miserable and everything could end but that it was okay.

Kate was in a newly built house, a warm home in a quiet, soggy town. Her son was seventeen and not showing any signs of leaving his comfortable room for a flat with his friends. But he was still at school so Kate supposed these days it was normal. She watched a nature documentary and passed time. She didn't smoke when she drank anymore. She didn't rip open the windows to hear a city pounding away in her ears. They had a tan lounge-suite. There were no mice. Her car was at the shop, getting new tyres. The guys at the auto shop would just put the new tyres straight on without calling about the price because they knew she wouldn't care. She almost missed the feeling of odd second hand tyres wobbling on the open road.

The turtles on the documentary hurtled towards the water, tripping over their fins. The first reached the water and was hit by a wave that sucked it up and spat it out. It was too disoriented to react before the second wave hit it. The narrator told her few would make it to adulthood. The camera dipped underwater to show the tiny bodies flipping and flopping in the currents.

Kate went and washed her face, watched it contort in the clean bathroom mirror. So many doors were closed now. She sat back down on the couch and muted the TV. She thought of her old friends, pulling up the sheets, the freedom of a terrible house and not knowing what came next. After a while her son came home from school and she wiped her face and sat up straight and they watched the Young and the Restless together.

PENNY'S WEDDING

P enny was having a smoke in her wedding dress when they all got up for breakfast, sitting on the doorstep and tapping the ash in her bourbon. There were grass stains down the front of her dress and she welcomed them all to the breakfast hall with an airy wave of her hand. "They wouldn't let me in," she said. "But help yourself." She laughed.

They all piled their plates from the steaming silver trays and sat down to eat at the wooden benches. The owner of the campground came and stood at the end of one of the tables.

"Right," he said. "Who moved the tractor?"

The guests looked at each other.

"Someone broke into the tractor," he prompted. "Drove it around. Left it by the river." He was trembling with barely controlled anger.

"I'm sorry," one of the bride's uncles said. "We don't know anything about it."

"Yeah," said one of the groom's friends. "We don't know about it."

The owner looked at the table in silence for a moment. Then he turned and walked straight past Penny, who waved her drink at him.

"Please don't be mad!" she cried.

The dust stirred in front of one of the cabins as Penny's new husband finally got up. She waved her drink at him as well. He stomped into the hall to get some food and then sat at the table with his friends.

"You moved the tractor," one of them said.

"Oh yeah," he said.

Another man came into the shed and looked at everyone from the sides of his eyes as he piled his plate with glistening sausages and spaghetti. Everyone knew he loved Penny.

"He got in a fight," someone whispered.

"What was it about?"

The whisperer shrugged.

"Hey, come here!" one of them shouted. The man who loved Penny came over and put his food down. The spaghetti shuddered.

"What was the fight about?"

The man shrugged. "Don't remember."

The men ate.

Penny was singing. She was scraping her feet back and forth in the dust, raising clouds. Everyone ignored her.

WINTER FIRES

(Previously published in takahē)

T he bartender, better dressed than Elizabeth, looked at her while she ordered. The bar itself had green walls, plants growing from little pockets all the way up to the high ceiling. The tables were full of men and women in suits. Their ties were already loosened and the women sat on the stools with their heels hanging off their feet, tanned calves pulsing. Elizabeth found Harry at one of those tables, his face already pink. The girl on the stool next to Harry jumped lightly off so Elizabeth could sit beside him.

"I've left the car at the office again. You don't mind..?"

Of course she didn't. Elizabeth perched on her stool and held her glass of wine. She found patterns in the light grain of the table. Their conversation had nothing to do with her. The young businesswomen were uncouth, they swore and looked racy doing it. They oozed the power they expected to come into. Elizabeth felt pastel.

"Better get off," Harry said. He rolled his eyes over at Elizabeth, a skittish horse.

Elizabeth didn't think that was fair, but she *was* hungry. She always felt uncomfortable ordering dinner at those places, where the women threw back their pints of beer in their ivory blouses and ignored any food on the table.

Harry waited in the car while Elizabeth did groceries. She hesitated at the fresh produce section and then bought strawberries. She hummed as she bought chocolate drops.

"Look," Harry said, as soon as she finished her last mouthful of chicken breast and broad beans. "I've been thinking about what you said — about the trip." Elizabeth had been lonely, researching trips to Europe. She had imagined them both sitting at an Opera in Venice, Harry next to her in a dark suit. Her heart leapt.

"Look. it's just not going to fit."

I know, it's okay, thought Elizabeth.

"But I want you to go. You should go."

Stop there—

"In fact I think we should put things on hold."

Elizabeth began to cry. She wished she had never mentioned Venice.

"Look. I think you should go to your mother's for a couple of days."

Look. He was treating her like a hard sell.

"What about your car?" she said at the door, hoping.

"What? Oh, I'll get an uber," he said. He wasn't

even looking at her anymore.

When Elizabeth got in her car she realised the chocolate strawberries were cooling in the fridge. He would open it later and find them. She drove through the city lights.

She couldn't go to her mother's. "Your sister is doing *so* well," her mother had said to her sister. Katrina worked on a farm, like they all had. *Pulling tits*, Harry called it, even though the farm wasn't a dairy one. Now Elizabeth was in the city and Katrina wasn't and their parents were retired in a town house where they sat in a large chair each and read the mail and talked about their daughters.

And of course, Elizabeth had told her mother about Europe, had mentioned it as a *very soon perhaps* — as a — *Harry seemed excited.* It had been Elizabeth who had allowed her mother to circle suitcases in her daily paper pamphlets.

Elizabeth headed out on the highway, watched it narrow and the street lights spill over her car less and less often and then not at all, until it was just her and the crops and the silent wires along the fences.

Down Katrina's long gravel road Elizabeth had to stop twice and tuck her skirt into her underwear to lift the latches on the stock gates. Mud coated her soft ballet slipper shoes. When she let herself into Katrina's unlocked house it was cold and it smelled like a den. Elizabeth tried to light the fire but the weak flames just licked the sides of the kindling and died. She rooted through Katrina's drawers for some fleece pants, pulling them on over her work clothes (how long ago that seemed now). She looked in the freezer in the shed. There was mutton cut in vague lumps and wrapped in plastic bags and she pulled out a leg, brushed off some ice and put it in the oven. She sat on the couch and tried not to move too much. An ancient dog snuffled at the door and then nosed his way inside, closing his eyes and lifting his lip. Elizabeth would have ordered him out, but instead she bumped herself from the couch onto the floor and held out her arms. He crept forward and sighed and she breathed deep and the dog leaned his stinking body into her.

"Yuck," said Katrina, from the doorway. Her quad had roared up to the house, dogs on the back jumping on and off barking in excitement for the lights being on in the house. The old dog stiffened and rolled onto his back. Katrina stared at him with her lip raised. She did not mention Elizabeth's arrival.

Katrina went back outside to feed and kennel her dogs, leaving the mutt inside for Elizabeth. She came back carrying a plastic milk bottle.

"Tried to light the fire?"

Elizabeth smiled. When they were children it was the girls' job to light the fire before their parents roared up to the house in the dark with their own dogs, sodden and hungry. But the firewood was always damp, always cheap or chopped too late in the season. The only way the girls could get it to start was to melt something over the wood, something toxic and unmissable like rags, milk bottles, old shoes. They would have caught it if their parents had found out. But now their parents were warm in town and the girls found ways to care for themselves. The smell of plastic soon filled the lounge and the kindling, coated in thick bubbles, began to catch.

By the time they'd pulled the roast from the oven the house was sweltering. They ate with the windows open until their bellies swelled over their fleece pants.

In the morning the frost had set in outside and cold water ran down the insides of the walls. To save sitting around cold all day Elizabeth dressed in some of Katrina's warm clothes and joined her sister in feeding the dogs. As Elizabeth reached into the sack of dog food a rat ran up her arm, launched off her shoulder and away, its fat body heaving. Katrina laughed and laughed. Then she kicked one of the dogs, which had nosed too close.

Katrina never asked Elizabeth how long she planned to stay. They went grocery shopping and cruised the aisles, buying eggs, bread, cheese, milk. It was so easy. There was no deciding what to cook each night, keeping it fresh and interesting. The girls ate eggs and cheese on toast during the day and mutton and potatoes at night. They drank instant coffee. At night Elizabeth sat and looked forward to her first coffee of the next day.

They watched television. Movies played end on end. At work Elizabeth straddled the back of the quad behind Katrina with the dogs leaning up against her, Katrina gunning through wet grass straight at cows who stood and watched her come. The cows always moved, kicking their back legs out at the quad and dancing away on small hooves. They'd run a few metres, stop, ignore the open gate they were supposed to go through, and look back at the girls. The dogs squealed to be let off. But no dogs among the cows, who were pregnant and only wanted to watch the two curious skinny girls leaning out and waving their arms and shouting horrific curses at them, both sides enjoying the waving and the swearing as a break from their routines of quietude.

How could life have gotten so difficult? Elizabeth wondered.

She woke up on the fifth night to the sound of nails, then teeth, against wood. There was a frost and the rats were eating their way up through the floors. She went to the kitchen, got an aluminium cooking tray, laid it over the growing hole in the carpet. Katrina nodded at it as she walked past. "I'll get some bait from the shed," she said.

Harry called on the sixth day. He just wanted to know where to drop her stuff.

After the weekend the oldest dog had a seizure and died. Katrina brought it home from the vet wrapped in a blanket. They took the quad up to the highest part of the farm, leaning together in unison over the ruts. The hill looked out over the paddocks, the sheds, the pine, the lake. The sun shone cleanly, the air up on the top was cold. Elizabeth and Katrina dug a hole, warming up quickly, stopping to drink from bottles of beer between shovelfuls of dirt. Elizabeth told Katrina how the business-women drank pints and swore in the pubs, holding the big glasses in their thin hands. Katrina shook her head in disbelief. The girls were dirty and sweating in baggy T-shirts and when they lifted the dog they dropped tears onto the blanket where his claws and the tip of his nose hung out.

The sun dropped and they sat drinking beer with the mutt packaged up in dirt beneath them, wrapped in his old blanket. Stars came out before the sun was completely done and then just kept coming, an overwhelming number of pinpricks pressing down on them. The stags started to roar in the crops, closer and closer, their guttural howls working up the girls' spines, women squatting before great fires, feeding the flames against the noises in the dark.

ABOUT THE AUTHOR

Tiffany Allan

Tiffany Allan is a New Zealand author published in Antipodes, Mayhem, On the Premises, and Mindfood.

To keep up with Tiffany's upcoming publications you can sign up to her newsletter here: https://sendfox.com/tiff.allan

Or follow her on Instagram here: https://www.instagram.com/tiffanyallanwriterspage/

Or on Facebook: https://www.facebook.com/tiffanyallanwriterspage/

Printed in Great Britain
by Amazon